Under
the
INDIAN SUN

Under
the
INDIAN SUN

SARAH ROBERTS

PARTRIDGE
A Penguin Random House Company

To order additional copies of this book, contact
Partridge India
000 800 10062 62
orders.india@partridgepublishing.com

www.partridgepublishing.com/india

PROLOGUE

I T WAS A COLD, FROSTY morning in February when Annie drove to Mont Dora, Florida. The sun shone in the clear sky, and the small town looked like the picture on a postcard. Young children ran about on the sidewalks, bundled up in brightly coloured warm clothes. Lovers strolled in scarves and caps, holding hands. Old people went in and out of quaint shops, carrying groceries, stopping to greet and talk to each other on their way. It was like an animated advertisement for a holiday resort, only real. Annie did not notice any of these details though. Her heart was heavy, and it hurt to draw in every breath. She pressed her lips together in a flat line and drove on through the streets. She had been driving for more than two hours and desperately needed a break, but Becky's place was just round the corner, so she drove on.

Becky's house was small and painted white and red, with a thatched roof, like the other houses in the street. There was a small green lawn in front, surrounded by a white picket fence; the lake was at the back of the house. Annie pictured its serene, clear waters, with almost no waves at this time of the year. For a moment, she envied her friend's tranquil life and then immediately felt ashamed of her thoughts. Becky had had her share of tragedies and pain; she deserved whatever peace she had now.

As she pulled over in front of Becky's house, she thought maybe this was not a good idea after all. It had been almost three years since she had seen Becky. She almost turned the key again, but then the front door opened, and Becky burst out, arms flung wide in welcome. Three small dogs ran out as well, their furry bodies wiggling in ecstasy.

'Annie! Honey. Come in, come in. You are just in time for coffee.'

Too late now, Annie thought as she was engulfed in a bear hug before they all went in.

Half an hour later, Annie pushed her plate away with a blissful sigh, wiping the corners of her mouth with the crisp white napkin. Breakfast was delicious, with freshly baked bread and bacon and eggs done to perfection. Becky had always had a way with food. Taking a sip from the freshly brewed coffee, Annie thought, *It just might work out after all*.

'That was awesome, Becky,' she said.

'It was nothing.' Becky dismissed it with a sweep of her hand. 'It felt good to cook for somebody other than myself for once. Now tell me, what do you plan to do? Shall we go out and do some shopping? Or you might want to have some rest,' she finished cautiously.

'No rest,' Annie reassured her. 'I feel like going out. Maybe I'll enjoy the lake this afternoon.'

'Sure. Whatever you like, honey.'

The dogs snoozed under the kitchen table. It was warm and cheerful inside the kitchen, like the rest of the house.

The table was covered in red-and-white gingham cloth, a bunch of flowers stuck inside an old teapot at the centre. The copper kettle gleamed, ready on the oven; the place smelled of bread and coffee. Annie felt herself relax.

Later, they had lunch at a lakeside restaurant. The fish was local catch, and the proprietor seemed to know Becky, so they had the house wine to go along with the fish, which Annie found to be surprisingly good.

'How are you holding up, sweetie?' Becky asked her over lunch.

Annie did not pretend to not understand. 'It was bitterly painful at first, you know? It's not easy giving up on a relationship of fifteen years.'

'I know. I felt my life was over when Harry left me. But trust me, it gets better after a while.'

'Yeah. It already feels like it. One more day here, and I'll definitely be on the mend.' Annie laughed. She took a sip of her wine and then said, 'Somehow this time it feels worse. You'd think that after the first time and with years of maturity behind you, you're better equipped to handle a divorce and a relationship. But I felt a lot less pain with Tim.'

'You were barely nineteen then. Both of you. I suspect feelings at that time in our lives are not that deep, you know?'

Annie nodded in agreement. 'That and also the fact that we divorced after eight years, but this time, Zack and I were together for more than ten years. It was a whole life I had built around him. Now that he's gone, I don't know what to do with the rest of me. It feels as if half of me were missing.' Sudden tears rolled down her cheeks.

Becky put down her fork and leaned over to wrap her arms over Annie's shoulder. 'Aw, honey, you will be over it.

I promise. Life is not over yet. Not by a long shot. You will find somebody. You mark my words. You will.'

They went to the local market after lunch, where Becky insisted on buying provisions for dinner. They argued over it.

'If you cook all the time, when will we go out?' Annie said.

'I love to cook. We will find ample time to go out. I plan to pack a picnic for us tomorrow, first thing in the morning, and I plan to pack a cake,' Becky retorted, laughing.

That set the mood for the rest of the weekend. Annie explored the small town, enjoying the crisp chill in the air. Miami never got that cold, and she was enjoying the winter air. Sometimes Becky joined her. Most people knew her; they would come up to say hi. The local shops had beautiful touristy pieces, little wall plaques, shot glasses with drink recipes, pens, playing cards with the map of Mount Dora on the back, and finally some home-made jams and jellies, which Annie thought would be good little gifts for her friends. Annie picked up quite a few. After her little shopping spree, they headed home to have dinner by the lakeside, watching the sun go down from Becky's backyard. The whole time had a dreamlike quality, which Annie knew was only for a brief period. But she didn't mind. She felt at peace after a long time.

'I wish you had come for a longer stay,' Becky said, watching Annie pack her things. She was to leave the next morning.

'I do too, but I have things to do back home.'

'What things? You are not working now.'

Annie used to work in the finance sector but was now semi-retired, doing freelance consultant jobs.

'You are your own boss. You can take time off when you like,' Becky continued.

Annie snapped shut her overnight case and sat on the bed. She looked thoughtful.

'Annie? Is there something you are not telling me?'

Annie looked up. She had an odd smile on her lips.

'Well? What is it?' Becky sounded tense.

Annie laughed. 'Don't be scared. It's nothing important really. It's just that—I am going to India later this year.'

'What? And that is not important? When did you plan this? How will you manage? When are you going? Tell me everything.'

Annie laughed. 'I planned this some time back. I am going in November. They say that is the best time to visit as the rains are over by then. There is this tour package that I have joined, and they will manage everything for me.'

'Are you sure, baby? Because it seems a bit—I don't know—far. You know?'

'Of course it is far. That is why I planned this.' Annie grew sober suddenly. 'I am tired of moping around. I need a change. I have always wanted to go to India, and the opportunity opened up, and I took it. First, it was my job—I had to build up my career. Then Zack was not interested in going too far from home, so I held back.' She bit her lower lip, pondering. 'You know, in hindsight, I realize that I held a lot of things back so that I could accommodate him.'

'Yes, you did,' Becky said softly. Annie darted a guilty look at her. They had been friends since high school, but of late, Annie had been neglecting their friendship a bit; Zack did not like Becky and her independent ways. But Becky did not look judgemental; she understood. She had always understood Annie. 'But if you are sure about this, then I am very happy for you. It's time you had some happiness—you have earned it.'

CHAPTER 1

A FEW MONTHS LATER, ANNIE DISEMBARKED from the jet at the Delhi International Airport. It was almost noon, and even though it was almost winter, it felt hot. She had been travelling for almost three days now, stopping briefly in London. Her eyes felt gritty from lack of sleep, and she wished fervently for a warm shower. But the journey was not yet over. She had to clear immigration and customs, both of which entailed long lines, and then there was the baggage retrieval.

Annie believed in travelling light, but she did not know what to expect from the Indian weather, so she had packed several items of clothing suitable for all conditions. Now, laden with three oversized bags, which she piled up on a trolley, she left the airport. Annie hoped she would not have to wait too long for the tour bus that was scheduled to pick her up. There was a line there as there were more members of the tour group waiting as well. Sighing, she got in line and wondered again whether she had done the right thing. Then she saw the bus driver waving frantically at her.

As soon as the bus rolled out of the airport, Annie was assaulted with a cacophony of sensations far different from home: a riot of colours and smells, dusty roads, and scenes of people in their ethnic dresses. Everything seemed a jumble of sights and sounds, which she felt ill-equipped to handle in her exhausted state. It was a relief to reach her hotel and seek the air-conditioned comfort inside.

After Annie checked in, a bellboy led her up to her room, which was tidily furnished. The air conditioner hummed softly, and some floral fragrance soothed her tired and jangled nerves. She tipped the bellboy with a smile of thanks and flopped down on the soft, inviting bed. *I'll rest for a while, then shower, and look up some lunch*, she thought before drifting off to a deep sleep.

When she woke up, it was dark outside. Her head felt heavy, and her mouth was dry. She stumbled out of bed and opened the closest suitcase, snatching a fresh T-shirt and a pair of shorts before bolting to the bathroom. After washing away the grime in warm water, she felt much better, and when she emerged a few minutes later into the bedroom, she felt hungry. There was a menu on the bedside table. Most of the food was unfamiliar, so she settled for some chicken soup and a sandwich, which she ordered to be brought up to the room. Exploring could wait another day, she decided.

Her gaze fell on her cell phone. She bit her lip, pondering what to do. It seemed such a huge step. What had seemed the most natural thing back home seemed like a gigantic, bold step now that she was in India. Suppose he thought she was easy? She suddenly wished Becky were there—she would know what to do. But Becky was thousands of miles away on the other side of the Atlantic; she didn't even know about this relationship. Annie had never told her.

With hesitant fingers, she took her cell phone, scrolling down for the number she was looking for. Taking a deep breath, she punched the number and then held her breath as she listened for the other side to pick up. She could hear her heart beating; maybe calling him was a bad idea. But she held on.

After a few rings, he answered. His deep voice made Annie shiver. She had felt like this for the last few months. Just the sound of his voice excited her.

'Hello?'

With an effort, Annie steadied her voice before speaking. 'Ashok. Hi.'

'I am so glad that you have arrived safely.' Then he suddenly sounded concerned. 'You *have* arrived, haven't you? You are not calling from home?'

'No, I have arrived. I landed earlier today.'

'Great. I would love to see you. When can we meet?'

'You tell me. I am on vacation. I should be free for the next few days until my tour begins.'

'That is great. I will call you later. Right now I am on duty, and I am very busy here in the restaurant, so I cannot talk much longer. I get off at two in the morning, and I shall call you after that if that's okay with you.'

'Okay. Goodnight.'

'Goodnight, Annie.'

Annie flung the phone on the bed and flopped over, stretching her arms over her head as her thoughts took her back to how she had met Ashok. She got to know Ashok while looking for an upscale restaurant in Delhi to have dinner on the last night of her tour. He was the assistant manager of the restaurant she had decided on. Annie then contacted the restaurant to make arrangements for the night that she wanted along with some special requests. She was put into contact with Ashok by the general manager who was going on vacation and couldn't work with Annie on her reservations. After a period of time of going back and forth during the preparation, Annie and Ashok had become close. Annie found him witty and fun, but he had his sensitive side as well. After Zack, Ashok was a balm to her wounded soul. She felt she could talk to him about anything and everything, and he felt the same—they were both wonderful listeners. Annie never once felt self-conscious as she talked about her divorce, her disenchantment with men, her children, and her family. Ashok soon opened up to Annie about his ambitions and dreams and his hope to one day leave India and seek greater opportunities. They both listened patiently to each other. And now—in a few hours—they were going to see each other for the first time.

There was a knock at the door; her dinner had arrived. She sat on the bed, watching television and ate her dinner. About midnight, Ashok called to say he would come over after he got off work, which would be around two in the morning. But Annie knew he would be tired and told him to go home. She suggested they meet in the morning.

It was barely light when Annie woke up the next morning. She lay on the bed, staring at the ceiling for some time, confused at first. The surroundings seemed unfamiliar; then she remembered. She sat up on the bed, excited, eager to take in as much as possible of the new place. Carefully pulling back the heavy curtains at the long windows, she peeked out. All she could see was the street below, like a smooth black snake lying still under the streetlights, which were still on. There was nobody on the street. Disappointed, she moved away and sat on the bed. The hotel was quiet at that early hour of the day. It would be at least an hour or so before the day began.

Sighing, she decided she would go back to sleep and went under the covers again, but sleep would not come. Maybe it was the new place, or maybe it was the time difference, but she was simply too awake. After a few restless minutes, she gave up and got out of bed again. After brushing her teeth, she took a quick shower and changed into a pair of white cotton trousers and a yellow frilly top, for the day promised to be fine. Then she went downstairs.

The lobby was deserted. The receptionist, a young man in his twenties, dozed at the desk.

'Good morning,' Annie said pleasantly.

'Good morning, ma'am,' said the young man, quickly awakened.

'I just wondered—might I take a stroll outside? The weather is fine, and I would like some exercise.'

'Yes, of course. Just do not go outside the gate.'

'Oh, but I thought I would walk down the street. I have to get out of the gate for that.' Annie was puzzled.

The reception clerk looked nervously towards the front gate. 'It is not very safe to go out on your own, ma'am. Is there anybody with you?'

'I am on my own.'

'Why don't you stroll inside, and then you can visit our gym if you want to exercise.'

'Maybe I will go to the gym now,' Annie said. 'Where is it?'

'It is closed right now. It opens at nine, so you have to wait till then.'

Annie gave up. 'Maybe I will go and sit out in the garden after all.'

The clerk looked relieved. 'Yes, ma'am.'

'And could you please not call me ma'am?'

'Yes, ma'am.'

Annie walked off towards the garden without another word. But once outside, her mood lifted. There was a light, cool breeze that brought in the fragrance of some tropical flower she knew not what. The lawn had been recently watered, and the grass looked fresh and green. The white rattan chairs with their pastel cushions looked inviting. She sat on one chair with a sigh of appreciation. It was so peaceful and quiet. As she sat there, she gradually became aware of sounds she had not heard before. Birds chirped on the branches overhead. Carts began to come out on the streets, their bells tinkling. She could hear singing from a temple not far from the hotel. Suddenly she was overwhelmed with a smoky smell; white smoke rose in a plume on the other side of the wall. Annie sat up, alarmed.

'Is there a fire out there?' she asked an old man who seemed to be the gardener. He was wearing a green uniform and carrying a watering can.

'Yes, madam,' he replied respectfully.

'Well then, call the fire department!' Annie was taken aback at the man's apparent lack of concern.

'Yes, madam,' he said and disappeared at the back of the building. Annie got up from her chair and went in as well.

The clerk at the desk was still there. He looked up as Annie strode in.

'There is a fire outside,' Annie announced.

Without a word, the man rushed outside to look. Annie followed him; he stood there, frowning, puzzled.

'A fire, you said?'

Annie pointed at the thick smoke still rising from beyond the wall. 'Oh. No, no. No fire. It is the tea stall vendors out there, setting their *chula* alight.' Seeing Annie's look of incomprehension, he elaborated. 'You know. Coal oven they cook in those. Make tea and snacks and sell them. They start the ovens at daybreak, put coal in, and . . .'

'I got it,' Annie said. She felt silly but also curious. 'You use coal for cooking?'

'Not us. We have electric ovens. Those are roadside stalls. For poor people, you know.'

'I see,' Annie said. 'Well, thank you, and sorry for bothering you.'

'No, no, ma'am. No bother.'

'Please call me Annie. Ma'am makes me feel so ancient.'

The clerk smiled at last. 'Okay. Madam Annie.'

Annie rolled her eyes. 'What is your name?'

'Raj.'

'Well, Raj, I shall take that stroll after all, seeing that the fire is not a dangerous one to worry about, I shall be back for breakfast. Say, about eight?'

CHAPTER 2

As Annie let herself out of the gate of the hotel, she glanced around curiously. Suddenly it seemed that the street was full of life—old people bundled up and strolling by, little children hurrying along in their school uniforms, bags and flasks dangling from their backs, traders and shopkeepers busily opening up their stores. She located the tea stall by the corner of the street; a coal oven with a large blackened kettle on top of it hissed away on the pavement. She was once again assailed by a riot of sounds, smells, and colours. She took a few tentative steps before turning and going back into the courtyard of her hotel.

It was almost breakfast time anyway, so Annie went to the dining room.

She was confused again as she looked at the menu. Most of the foods were unfamiliar. She beckoned a passing waiter.

'Tell me what is this . . . *puri*?

'It is bread.'

'Ah. Bread. Bring me some—and eggs please.'

'Sure, madam.'

A little later, she was presented with some round oily fried pancakes with a bowl of vegetables. A couple of fried eggs accompanied her platter.

'What is this?' Annie asked, perplexed.

'Puri, madam. You ordered?'

'But you said bread.'

'This is bread. Indian bread,' the waiter assured her with a smile.

Annie was at a loss as to what to do when she heard a familiar voice, a deep baritone. 'Annie?'

She turned around to see a young man standing, smiling down at her. Her breath caught. She had seen him in the images he had sent her, but he was much more forceful in person. Ashok was five foot nine with flashing dark eyes and thick blue-black hair, a bit on the shorter side. A cream shirt, which showed his lightly tanned throat, and a pair of khaki trousers made him look cool and composed.

'Ashok?'

Annie stood up. Not sure if she should hug him in public, she instead outstretched her hand for a handshake. His hand was warm and gentle as they lingered for a moment.

'May I sit?' Ashok raised an eyebrow in amusement. Annie suddenly felt gauche and uncertain.

'Yes—yes, of course. Sorry.'

Ashok pulled up a chair and sat down.

'Would you like some breakfast?' Annie asked.

'I have eaten, thank you. I don't mind some tea though.' He beckoned a waiter and requested some tea before turning back to her.

'So we meet, finally.' He smiled. He had strong white teeth, Annie noticed.

'Yes, we do.'

'You like puri?' That black eyebrow went up again.

Annie gave a small rueful laugh. 'I am not sure what this is. I was told this is bread, but it doesn't seem anything like any bread I have had.'

'Well, these are Indian flatbreads, deep-fried. You are to have them accompanied with the vegetables. See, like this.'

Ashok tore a small portion of the puri and a spoonful of the veggies in the bowl and offered them to Annie. She took a small bite from his hands; he put the rest of it in his mouth. Somehow, the act of chewing food together, taken from the same portion, seemed intimate to Annie. She laughed a little awkwardly, feeling self-conscious. But the food was delicious, even if she was not used to so much spice first thing in the morning. She polished off the rest of it, leaving the eggs aside.

Tea arrived. 'So what are your plans for the coming days?' Ashok asked as Annie poured.

'Well, my tour operator will be here in about an hour. I will know the details of the tour plan then. But I think we shall spend the first couple of days sightseeing locally by going to Old and New Delhi, see one or two of the famous temples and the local markets, then we shall start the tours of the other places.'

'Makes sense. That way, you can familiarize yourselves gradually to the chaos that is India,' Ashok said with laughter in his voice. Annie smiled. The more she saw of him, the more she liked him. After they had finished having tea, Annie made her excuse and went to one of the bathrooms on the ground floor.

After going in, she splashed some cold water on her face, then grabbed a handful of tissues from the rack and dabbed her face. She peered into the mirror, taking a critical look at her face: a brown face, with curly hair that hung to her back and wisps of it falling on her forehead, straight nose, full lips, brown wide-set eyes with eyebrows that arched naturally. She peered closer; were those lines on her forehead? She pursued her lips, applied some blush from her purse, and stepped back to have another look. She needed more colour on her lips. Luckily, she was never without her lipstick, and after applying the soft coral colour, she felt she could face Ashok now. His handsome looks made her feel inadequate. *Well, this is the best I have in me*, she thought, shrugging before going out.

Her cell phone was ringing by the time she reached her table. Fishing it out of her purse, she saw it was her tour operator. Ashok waited, his eyes smiling at her while she talked on the phone.

'That was Niraj, our tour operator,' Annie explained after she finished her call. Ashok nodded.

'Do you start sightseeing today?' he asked.

'Yes. In about an hour, the bus will come and pick me up from the hotel and afterwards will drop me here as well. We shall have lunch and dinner outside, it seems.'

Ashok looked at his watch. 'Well, I have to make a move myself. I have a meeting later in the day, and I have to prepare the paperwork before I go there.' He stood up, pushing back his chair. Annie wished he could stay a little longer. She stood up as well.

'I think I shall get ready for the tour as well. What do you think I should carry? Is it going to be hot outside?'

'I don't think so, no. Not too hot. I would carry some drinking water though if I were you. Water gets contaminated quite easily in the tropics, I am afraid.'

'Right. I shall carry a bottle with me then.'

'And I really have to go now. It was good seeing you, Anita.' He liked to call her that when he teased her.

'Please call me Annie.'

'See you later then, Annie. I will call you. Please feel free to call me any time if you need anything. It will be my pleasure to come to any help you need.' Ashok held out his hand, and Annie clasped it in a brief handshake before stepping back. He had a strong grip, his palm dry and pleasant to touch.

Annie went back to her room and changed into a long skirt that fell to her ankles. It was of various shades of orange and rust. She teamed it up with a brown sleeveless blouse in soft cotton. After much consideration, she pushed her feet into a pair of canvas flat pumps and tied up her curls in a leather thong. Her make-up was very little, but she was careful enough to use sunscreen liberally on her face and arms. Collecting her purse, she went out of her room to wait for the bus to arrive.

CHAPTER 3

THE BUS ARRIVED AT THE appointed time. Annie felt a small shiver of excitement as she went on board the bus; this was her first trip so far away from home and on her own. The tour guide, Niraj, greeted her with a warm smile.

'Hello, Anita, ma'am. We are all so pleased to meet you.'

Annie smiled her greeting and then headed for the back of the bus.

The bus was beautifully decorated with ribbons, yellow flowers, and lights. After all, it was Diwali; that was why Annie was there—for this special celebration of lights. She found a seat and sank gratefully on to it. Her neighbour was a sweet elderly lady—probably European, she deduced. The bus started as Niraj introduced everybody. There were people from all over: the United States, Canada, England, Australia, and South Africa. And then there were a few people from India as well. As the bus meandered through the busy streets of Delhi, Annie learned that the part of the city they were to visit that day was the old part of Delhi. The bus was spacious and air-conditioned, for which she was thankful, and the darkly tinted windows offered protection from the sun as well as the busy streets, which Annie found chaotic. The houses were decorated with marigold garlands, their bright yellow petals contrasting sharply with green leaf wreaths.

'Diwali is only a day away,' Niraj explained. 'The houses are decorated for the festival.'

'What is Diwali?' one of the tourists asked.

'Well, it is a festival of light and sound. Hindus decorate their houses and light lamps and burst crackers. We also exchange sweets,' Niraj replied.

The first stop for the tourists was the Birla Temple. It was at the heart of the city and dedicated to the Hindu goddess Lakshmi and her divine lord Narayan, Niraj explained. The temple, which was three storeys high, was enchantingly covered with carvings depicting Hindu mythology. Apart from the main temple of Lakshmi and Narayan, there were smaller temples in the complex, with shrines dedicated to Lord Shiva, Lord Ganesha, and Lord Buddha. Annie found the idol of Ganesha quaint; he had the head of an elephant and the body of a man. Apparently, he loved to eat, or so Niraj claimed with a smile, which explained his rotund build.

As they came back to the bus, Niraj remarked that it was one of the very few Hindu temples in India that allowed non-Hindus in. Apparently, Mahatma Gandhi had inaugurated the temple, and he did it on the condition that it would not be restricted to any caste or religion.

'You mean that if I want to worship any deity, I am not allowed because I am not a Hindu?' Annie asked.

'Alas, I am sorry to say, madam, but you may not,' Niraj replied with a sad shake of his head.

'That is ridiculous. It restricts my rights as an individual. Don't you think?' Annie was aghast.

'It is the Hindu faith,' her elderly neighbour said softly. 'You cannot worship unless you are a Hindu, and you have to be born a Hindu, you know.'

'Whatever. I think it is quite unfair,' Annie mumbled. But her spirits lifted at the next stop. It was another temple but of a different faith.

'This is a Gurudwara, which is the temple of the Sikhs,' Niraj announced as they came down from the bus. It was considerably hot by this time, and as they came out of the air-conditioned interiors, a few remarked on how uncomfortable they felt in the heat. But Annie thought it was pleasant; she was more used to the tropical climate than some of the Europeans. But they had to cover their heads with scarves anyway. It seemed that the Sikh temple did not allow people in with their heads uncovered. They also had to take off their shoes and leave them at a shoe-minding room. Some of them did not have scarves with them; they were provided with some yellow cloth from the Gurudwara to cover their heads. There was a pond outside, where they dipped their feet before trudging in.

Annie spent some time in the temple's community kitchen. It was a huge affair where volunteers were preparing large amounts of lentil soup and chapattis (Indian flatbread) in numerous gleaming ovens. All had their heads covered and were barefoot. The community kitchen was open to all sections of society, she learned from a volunteer, be it rich or poor, irrespective of caste, religion, or nationality. She was tempted to taste a little of the food but restrained herself out of respect. There was also a school, an art gallery, a library, and a hospital within the temple complex. They went through all of them, marvelling at the sheer amount of community service undertaken by one small religious temple.

Afterwards, they went outside and lit candles on the decorated alcoves as it was very near Diwali, and then it was time for lunch.

Lunch was at a restaurant with an unpronounceable name. Annie was apprehensive about the food; the memory of the fiasco at breakfast was still fresh in her mind. But the interior of the air-conditioned place and the neat ambience felt reassuring. They were all quite famished after the tour, and it was obvious that the staff was expecting them. The tables were laid ready, and as soon as they took their places, they began to serve. There was no need to order anything as the tour operator had arranged it, and the menu had been fixed already. Some of the tourists wondered what went into the recipes; the food was surprisingly delicious.

'Anita, madam, you must be familiar with the food. I heard that you are Indian in origin,' Niraj remarked.

Annie shook her head. 'I must say this is all unfamiliar to me. Back home, we do eat Indian food, but the spices and herbs are so different here. I love this.' She smiled. Just then, her cell phone rang.

It was Ashok. Annie's heart skipped a beat, and then she felt ashamed of her reaction. She was a mature woman, and she had no business feeling this way about a man who was younger than her by at least a dozen or more years, she told herself sternly as she flipped the phone open to take the call.

'Annie? Ashok.'

'Yes, Ashok. Is your meeting over already? I hope it went well.'

'Oh, it was all right. What are you doing now?'

'We are having lunch. Then we will do a bit of shopping, I think. At least that's what Niraj says.'

'Niraj?'

'Our tour guide.'

'Oh. I was wondering what you are doing tomorrow.'

'Well, more sightseeing. We start at nine, right after breakfast.'

'All right. I shall see you at breakfast then. Is that okay with you?'

Annie was a bit disappointed; she had hoped to see him for dinner, but she didn't let it show. 'It is okay. Absolutely.'

Ashok seemed to hesitate for a moment, and then he said, 'I would have seen you at dinner tonight, but I have to have dinner with my aunt. She came down for a visit from Punjab, and I can't avoid that.'

'It is absolutely okay. You must see your aunt, Ashok. See you tomorrow at about eight?'

'Okay. See you too.'

Ashok rang off. As Annie put the phone back in her purse, she was unaware of the little smile around her lips. The rest of the day went well. They went to a shopping mall at the heart of the city and dispersed, with instructions by Niraj to return to the bus after ninety minutes. Annie explored the shops to her heart's content, admiring the colourful saris and dresses in heavy sequin work. There were shops of well-known European labels as well, such as Gucci, Armani, and Versace. She particularly liked a Nina Ricci dress; it was deep purple, which set off her dark looks. It was deceptively simple in cut, the material draping her lush figure in lustrous silk, falling just below her calves. She fell in love with it, and the price seemed to be not that much when converted into dollars. Afterwards, she looked for some matching shoes as well and finally settled for some black-and-purple strappy sandals. She wanted to buy some saris as well, but as she didn't know much about them, she left it for later. *Maybe I shall get someone local like Niraj to help me choose*, she thought. She also bought some gift items for home. Looking at her watch, she saw there was just enough time for one quick coffee. Locating a coffee shop inside the mall, she went in.

By the time she came back to her hotel, she was too tired to go down for dinner. She rang for some sandwiches, had a quick shower, cleaned her teeth, and was asleep almost as soon as her head hit the pillow.

It was early when she awoke the next day. She could hear the bells tinkling on the road below her window, and she knew that the day had started. Sure enough, she could spot the plume of white smoke from the coal oven when she peeked outside. It was already time to get ready for the day. Picking up a mint-green sleeveless jumpsuit in soft cotton, she went to the bathroom. When she came out, she brushed her hair and pulled it back from her face with the leather tie and put a slim leather belt around her waist. She glossed her lips in coral, put on light eye make-up, and looked at herself in the mirror.

You'll do. You clean up not bad, she thought. Then after pushing her feet into her flat strappy Grecian sandals, she collected her purse and went out.

Breakfast was already being served when she entered the dining room. She checked her watch; it was quarter to eight. She was early as Ashok was to be there at eight. She sat at a table by the large French window, looking out at the garden.

'Breakfast, madam?'

'Thank you. I am waiting for my friend to arrive.' She smiled. The waiter discreetly withdrew. There were very few people at this hour, she saw. At the far end, there was an elderly gentleman who was pushing around a plateful of fruits. She noticed a group of young men, probably sales executives, in an animated discussion over toast and eggs. Then she saw him.

Ashok stood at the doorway as he tried to locate her. She utilized the brief moment to drink him in. He was wearing light-blue denims and a dark cotton polo. His feet were clad in casual light-brown loafers. Annie thought he looked too handsome. His eyes searched the room and lit up as they landed on her. He started to make his way towards her through the length of the dining room.

'Good morning,' he said with a smile.

Suddenly Annie felt breathless. 'Good morning,' she somehow managed to get out.

God, I sound as if I were croaking. He must be thinking I am awfully gauche, she thought. But Ashok did not seem to notice. He pulled a chair and sat at her table.

'You have already eaten?' he asked.

'No. No, I was waiting for you. After yesterday, I am not sure what to order,' Annie replied with a nervous laugh. *Did I just giggle?*

Ashok was laughing too. 'I recommend the *aloo paratha*,' he was saying, going through the menu, his lips pursed. He looked up. 'Tea or coffee?'

'Coffee, thank you. What is aloo . . . paratha?'

'Well, it is stuffed Indian flatbread. The stuffing is of potato, which is *aloo*, hence the name.' Seeing Annie's look of hesitation, he reassured her, smiling. 'Try it. I think you will like it.'

'Okay then.'

Ashok beckoned a waiter and placed the order.

'Now then, tell me how you are liking India.'

'Well, it is too early to say. I have been here only since yesterday. But whatever I have seen so far, I think I like it.'

'You think?' Ashok teased gently.

'Hmm. There is chaos as you had warned me. And it is dusty and very crowded. But I like the colours on the street—everybody, especially the women and children, is so draped in colours. And people are friendly.'

Their food arrived. For the next few minutes, there were not many words as they concentrated on their breakfast. Despite her misgivings, Annie found the *paratha* to be quite tasty. She helped herself to some yogurt that was provided with it but declined the pickles. 'Too spicy, I think, for breakfast,' she said.

'So what are your plans for today?' Ashok asked her, leaning back and taking a sip from his coffee.

'Well, let's see. The bus arrives at nine thirty, and then we start a tour of the old part of the city. Niraj tells us that has quite some history.'

'Tell you what.' Ashok put down his cup and leaned forward, elbows on the table. 'Why don't you come away with me? I can give you a guided tour of Old Delhi. We can explore the city if you like, and that way, you can stop and return if you feel tired.'

'Can I? But what about the bus?'

'I am sure they will not mind. Unless you'd prefer that, of course.'

'No. No, I wouldn't prefer that. Yesterday was quite tiring, hopping from one place to another. I would much rather explore at my own pace, I think.'

'Great. Then let me talk to the front desk. We shall leave a message for your tour guide, and you can talk to him later.'

Ashok got to his feet and strode towards the reception desk. Annie suppressed a thrill of sheer joy. *There is no need to read too much into the offer. He is just being polite to a foreigner in the city, that's all*, she told herself. But at the same time, a tiny voice in her heart could not help but wonder. Surely it meant something that he was ready to spend a day—a whole day—with her. He would not offer that if he were merely being polite. At least he did not dislike her company, she reassured herself.

Ashok came back. 'Are you ready to leave? We can start right now if you want to.'

'I am ready,' Annie said as she stood up and picked up her tote bag.

CHAPTER 4

ONCE OUTSIDE, SHE SCANNED THE car park for his car.
But Ashok strode towards the back of the building,
leaving Annie to wait in the portico. A minute later, she
heard the roar of the engine; he came back wearing a helmet,
his visor lifted to show his face, riding a motorcycle.

'I hope you are okay with a bike,' he said as he offered
her a helmet.

'I am okay,' Annie said as she strapped on the helmet. The
truth was she had been on a bike before, but in India, it was
something very scary. But she was not about to confide that.

'The thing is, parking the car is such a problem in
Delhi. I find riding a bike much easier.'

Annie got on the back of the bike, firmly clasping him
by his middle. She immediately became aware of the scent
of his skin and flushed slightly, but Ashok did not see that.

'Don't you find the weather a bother? I mean, it is hot.
And then there is the rain.'

'Actually,' said Ashok as he carefully rode down the
driveway of the hotel, 'I find the bike to be freeing. It makes

me happy to feel the air on my face and the sun on my back. I take out the car when it rains or when I am sure that I will be able to get parking.'

They eased out into the main road, where he picked up speed. Annie was tense for the first few minutes, but after some time, she relaxed. It was indeed fun, she discovered, to feel the air through her hair. She felt unrestricted and soon was enjoying the bike ride as they meandered through narrow lanes and sped on broad streets. They went to see the tomb of the Mughal king Humayun. Annie remarked that it looked quite similar to the Taj Mahal.

'But of course I have seen only pictures of the Taj,' she said. 'Maybe I am hopelessly off the mark.'

'You are not, actually,' Ashok said. 'This is known as the precursor to the Taj Mahal. The two are quite similar in structure, though of course Taj Mahal is bigger and entirely white, giving it an ethereal beauty.'

They went to see the Qutb Minar. It was impressive in its height, all of 72.5 metres, Annie learned from Ashok. It had 379 stairs to the top.

'You have a great view of the city from the top,' Ashok said. So they climbed the stairs.

'Do you know that Qutbuddin Aibak, after whom the tower is named, only finished the first storey in his lifetime?'

'No, I didn't. I am not sure who Qutbuddin Aibak is for that matter.' Annie laughed. She was starting to feel a bit breathless by then. The stairs were steep.

'Well, he was the one who started to build it.' Ashok shrugged. 'I am afraid I don't know much about him either. The rest of the tower was built over a period of time by his descendants.' They came to an open balcony, one of several, and decided to take a breather.

'You were right,' Annie said as they looked over the balustrade towards the landscape. 'The view is beautiful.'

'Wait till you go to the top.'

'Umm . . . I think I will take a bow here.'

'All right,' Ashok said easily. 'We take a little rest. Then we go down.'

They stared at the city with its crumbling buildings and narrow lanes in companionable silence for some time.

'Have you been to the top?' Annie asked suddenly.

'Uh-huh.'

'You like it there.' It was a statement, not a question. Ashok turned to her in surprise.

'You are right. Though *like* is not perhaps the right word. I love it there. It is a bit like riding my bike. You know?'

Annie nodded in agreement. She understood. 'Like you are free from boundaries.'

Ashok looked at her, startled, but Annie was looking out towards the skyline and didn't seem to notice.

They came down after some time. 'Are you hungry?' Ashok asked.

'I am, actually.'

'Okay then, let's have lunch.'

Annie was a bit apprehensive about the food; she was not sure her stomach would hold up against the entire spicy onslaught. As they came out into the main street, she suddenly noticed a McDonalds—right there in the middle of the city. She sighed.

'Fancy having a burger?' Ashok raised his voice against the wind. Without looking back, he had felt her sigh.

'You wouldn't mind?'

'Why should I? I love a burger as much as the next man.' He negotiated his bike and took a turn towards the restaurant.

They ordered burgers with extra-large fries and Cokes. Annie suddenly realized she had been craving familiar food, though she was not aware of it until she had a plateful of fries in front of her. Seeing her eye them eagerly, Ashok hid an amused smile.

They made small talk while eating. Ashok told her a bit about the history of Old Delhi—that it was originally known as Shahjahanabad, after the Mughal king Shah Jahan, when he moved his capital from Agra back here. Delhi had seen quite some turbulence and invaders in its time; only three of the fourteen gates of the city now survived. Courtiers, merchants, artists, and poets had once inhabited the narrow lanes of the older part of the city.

'But myths about the city go back to the times of the *Mahabharata*. It is believed that this was once the capital of the Pandavas. It was then called Indraprastha.'

'Really? I never knew all this.' Annie was fascinated.

'We shall visit the Jama Masjid after we finish lunch,' Ashok decided.

The Jama Masjid turned out to be a huge mosque— *masjid* meaning 'mosque'—and it was the main mosque from the time of Shah Jahan.

'It can hold up to 25,000 people at a time,' Ashok remarked as they reached it. At Annie's sceptical look, he shrugged. 'That's what I have been told, and I believe it.' But once they were near the gate, Annie was inclined to believe it. It was huge—in fact, a whole complex of domes and minarets. Annie thought it was almost like a city within the city. She remarked as much to Ashok, who inclined his head in agreement.

'They say that it took 5,000 labourers to finish the mosque. The estimated cost was about one million rupees in those times.'

'I can imagine that,' Annie agreed as they climbed up the crimson stairs and went through the gate—one of the three, Ashok said.

'On my god!' she said once she was inside the main congregation hall.

'Yes. I know. Do you know that the mosque can be seen from any region within a five-kilometre radius?'

'I can imagine it. This is awesome.'

They explored the insides for some time. 'I love the domes, even if they seem a bit like onions, I think. You know?'

Ashok laughed. A few of the faithful looked at him, annoyed. He lowered his voice. 'I do hope no one understands English here,' he said solemnly.

After some time, they went down the stairs. The steps served as stalls for various items, including books and eateries in the evening, Ashok explained. 'The western side sells poultry and meat, and the southern side sells books,' he said. 'Would you like to go the Red Fort? It is very near. No point in missing it, seeing that we are here.'

'Sure,' said Annie. 'I would love that. I have heard so much about it.'

The Red Fort was red. Annie was not sure what to expect, but she was taken in by the sheer beauty of the large red stone wall that surrounded the ancient fort.

'It's . . .' Annie gasped at a loss for words.

'Like it?' Ashok said, his eyes on her. Her attention was on the massive structure before her.

'It's amazing. Breathtaking.' She looked at him. 'What is on the other side?'

'Well, the river. The fort stands on the banks of Yamuna, the river that flanks Old Delhi on one side. Want to have a look?'

'Yes, please.'

Ashok shot her an amused glance.

The river was narrow, and its banks were piled high with all sorts of things—plastic sheets, old newspapers, cans, half-eaten food—and it stank. Annie fancied she even spotted flies buzzing at a place or two.

'Ugh!' She put a hand to her nose, grimacing. Ashok could not help but notice the delicate arch of her fingers. Then he saw the sheer disgust in her face and laughed.

'I should have warned you,' he said.

'Yes, you should have.'

'Not the pleasant riverfront you imagined, I am afraid,' Ashok said as they made their way back. 'Yet once it was one of the most important rivers of India.'

'Yes, I know. I have read much about the myth of Shri Krishna. I had such beautiful pictures in my mind.' Annie was thoroughly disappointed. 'Let's get out of here.'

They came around the corner to where Ashok had parked his bike. As they put their helmets on, Annie suddenly exclaimed, 'What's that?'

It was a type of tricycle pedalled by one in the front while two people sat behind.

'Oh, it's a rickshaw,' Ashok remarked. 'One of the cheapest modes of transportation in India.'

'I have heard about them. They are pulled by humans.'

'Pedalled. And even if humans operate it, it's not as bad as it looks.'

'I would like to try it,' Annie announced.

'Sure. How about tomorrow?' Ashok asked as they weaved into the crowded street.

'Great. Sure.' Dusk was descending upon the old city; streetlights were turned on. Annie thought the streets looked like a magic land, something straight out of *Harry Potter*, with their colours and lights, people and cows jostling each other for space, and loud noises. A loudspeaker blaring Hindi songs accompanied by louder music somehow added to the general din. There was a pleasant breeze; Annie caught a whiff of Ashok's cologne. It felt so intimate somehow. She flushed a bit, but thankfully, Ashok was fully concentrating in the traffic.

That night, as she got ready for bed, Annie suddenly realized that she had barely thought about the past few months the whole day. All she could recall of the day was a happy blur, a collage of sights and sounds and smells, and the feel of Ashok's hands on her waist as he helped her over a flight of broken steps on the riverfront, the smell on his shirt, a mix of cologne and skin, as she rode the back of his bike. She still had one day before she set out for Jaipur; suddenly she felt breathless with excitement. She couldn't wait for the day to begin so she could see Ashok again.

The next day dawned bright and chilly. Annie lay in bed for a few seconds, confused. It seemed that there was something that was about to happen; she just could not recollect what. Then she remembered. Ashok was coming over to pick her up. They would have breakfast together, and then he was to take her out for the day. She threw the covers and jumped out of bed.

Twenty minutes later, she peered at the mirror critically. She had on a pair of light-blue denims and a burnt-orange top. She eyed the boat neckline of the blouse; it had a delicate lace border. Was it too girlish? Suddenly she felt inadequate, self-conscious, and a bit sad. Maybe she was making a fool of herself; maybe what she felt was nothing but desperate wishful thinking of a middle-aged woman. But her figure was trim, and her complexion was clear. She looked closely; her eyelashes were good, thick and long. She had always been complimented on her eyelashes. Annie sighed and picked up her lip gloss. Then she slipped into a pair of tan low-heeled pumps and went out.

Ashok was already waiting when she came down. As soon as he noticed her, he stood up, his eyes lighting up. He was wearing a pair of denims too, but he had teamed it up with a cotton shirt in charcoal. His sleeves were turned up, showing his powerful forearms. As Annie approached, he pulled out a chair for her. For some reason, Annie liked it and smiled when she said, 'Forever polite, are you?'

Ashok shrugged as he too sat down. 'I certainly try.'

They had a sumptuous meal of grilled chicken sandwiches, fruits, and coffee and orange juice. Ashok remarked that it was very American to have coffee and orange juice together.

'Here we shall not have it like the way you do,' he said. 'We prefer tea, but even if we have coffee, juice is reserved for later in the day—or afternoon.'

'Really?' Annie took a hearty swig of the freshly squeezed juice. She eyed the fruit platter with relish. It contained cuts of melon, orange, bananas, pineapple, and so forth.

'That is one thing I like about you.'

'Only one?' Annie raised one eyebrow.

Ashok laughed. 'Well, one among many.'

'Hmmm. What is that?'

'You enjoy your food. It is very off-putting to be at the same table with somebody who picks at food.'

Maybe he thinks I am fat, Annie thought uncomfortably. But almost immediately, she knew Ashok meant what he said; he had such a clear look in his eyes. It was impossible not to take him at face value. A warm glow spread over her cheeks; she lowered her eyes, feeling uncharacteristically tongue-tied.

Later, they went out towards the older part of the city again as Annie wanted to explore. Ashok kept his bike under a shed where other people kept their bikes too; it seemed that one could keep bikes there for a fee. They walked for some time, Annie soaking in the scents and scenes of the narrow lanes until she felt tired.

'Can we take a ride on the rickshaw?'

'Sure.'

They travelled on a rickshaw that was coloured brightly in garish shades of yellow and green and pink, the hood over the passenger seat up to protect them from the sun. There was not much space in the passenger seat; it was a bit of a squeeze for Annie and Ashok. She could feel one side of his entire body—from shoulder to toes—press against her. She tried to look sideways, trying to gauge his reaction to the unexpected proximity, but he seemed quite oblivious to their forced intimacy. Annie wasn't sure whether to feel relieved or dejected.

'What are those?' she asked, pointing towards some roadside stalls with colourful merchandise. At first glance, they seemed like chocolate wrappings, small objects covered in shiny metallic wrapping paper. But Ashok said those were crackers. 'You know, for Diwali.'

'Oh? Can I have a look?'

They got down from the vehicle and went to the stalls. Annie looked closely at the brightly wrapped packages but could not make anything out of them. She looked back at Ashok, grimacing. 'I need your help here, I guess.'

After a few minutes, they were back on the rickshaw, with Annie carrying an armful of crackers and fireworks. She wanted to explore the quaint shops in the lanes, and after stopping the rickshaw for the nth time, they had to let go of it.

'How will we find the bike?' Annie was a little worried.

'Oh, I know where it is. We can always take something on our way back,' Ashok reassured her.

After a couple of hours of shopping, they stopped at a roadside eatery to sample some of the street food of Delhi. Annie was charmed by the fruit salad, known as *chaat*, sprinkled with tangy spice. Her eyes caught sight of a man and a sort of stand with a big covered pan on top of it. People surrounded him, eating something out of tiny paper bowls.

'What's that?' she asked, pointing.

'Oh, it is the mother of all street food,' Ashok replied with a twinkle in his eyes. 'We call it *golgappa*, but it has many other names throughout India. Want to try?'

'I am not sure. Will it be very spicy?' Annie's mouth was still smarting from the hot spice in the chaat.

'Come on, let's find out.'

Annie was not sure she liked the taste of the golgappa; it was a crispy sphere filled with spicy mashed potato and dipped in very sour tamarind gravy. She had to put it straight into her mouth; otherwise, it ran down her elbows, she found out, to her chagrin and Ashok's amusement.

'Ugh! It's messy!' She grimaced.

They wandered along the streets for some time, Annie peeping curiously inside curio shops; she was looking for small gifts to take back home. As she came out of a shop, she spotted a huge bull blocking the path on the pavement. People were simply going around it. Some even ran their hands down his back—for luck, Annie deduced. The bull ignored everything, standing still like a statue, munching a cabbage. A few other vegetables were set in front of him, presumably by reverent devotees. It was no use demanding that it be shooed away, Annie knew, as the Hindus in India revered bulls. But there was no way she could go around it; it was too huge. She looked up at Ashok helplessly.

'I can't go around it,' she confessed.

Ashok nodded. 'Hold my hand,' he offered. Annie took it gratefully. 'Okay, now follow me. There's nothing to be scared of. He is actually quite gentle, you know,' Ashok murmured. She took baby steps, taking care to stick close to Ashok as they gingerly went around the huge animal, taking care not to disturb it. Just as they were almost past it, the bull suddenly opened its eyes and made a grunting sound. The next thing Annie knew, the ground was far beneath her feet.

'Who—what?'

Ashok gently disengaged her arms from around his neck and put her back on her feet.

'We are past it. See?' he said softly. Sure enough, they were past the bull. It had closed its eyes again and was bunching blissfully, Annie noticed, not without a touch of resentment.

'Thank you. But what happened?'

'You were scared and . . .'

Annie understood and flushed warmly. 'Say no more. I made a fool of myself,' she groaned. She felt like digging a hole and crawling in; there was no way he would not think her a complete bimbo after this.

'No, no. I think the bull wanted to take a good look at you. And I don't blame him,' Ashok teased gently. 'I'd do anything to take a good look at a beautiful woman.'

'Please don't.' Annie started to walk away, averting her face. She needed to get away from him; she was beyond mortified.

Suddenly she was grabbed by her hand and spun around. 'I meant it. I think you are beautiful.' He lifted his hand and gently tucked back a strand of her hair. 'You are beautiful,' he said again before lowering his lips to hers.

Annie was too shocked to react for the first few moments, but then her mouth softened, almost unconsciously. His lips were warm, soft, and dry. He moved them back and forth, brushing against her lips before stepping back. 'Let's get back to the hotel,' he said with a smile in his eyes.

CHAPTER 5

THEY MADE THEIR WAY BACK to the hotel in silence. Ashok rode his bike through the crowded streets, Annie clinging to him. She inhaled deeply, taking in the scent she had come to associate with him. It was well past afternoon by the time they reached the hotel. Ashok parked the car without a word before they went up to her room, hand in hand. Annie closed the door behind them before turning to face him. Ashok stood still in the middle of the room. Annie suddenly felt hot and then cold all over. She seemed to be shivering. She took a tentative step forward; suddenly she was in Ashok's arms. He rained kisses on her face, nose, eyes, and mouth. Annie felt like weeping. Suddenly Ashok held her a bit away from him, looking down at her with concern.

'Annie?'

'I am sorry,' Annie said in a trembling voice, tears rolling down her cheeks. She was not sure why she was shivering. For the first time in her life, she felt so cherished. She tucked her face in his chest, suddenly bashful. Ashok laughed softly under his breath, his mouth on her hair. Slowly, he led her towards the bed in the middle of the room. Annie allowed herself to be led.

It was almost dusk when Annie opened her eyes; she had dozed off for a while. Turning her head, she saw Ashok on his stomach, one arm flung over her middle. She looked at his bare back for a while, admiring his broad shoulders before sitting up. Looking around, she noticed a faint glow inside the room. Curious, she threw the bedclothes off and padded off to the chair where she had her bathrobe neatly folded up. Shrugging into it, she went to the window and stared.

The whole street, the houses, the shops—in fact the whole neighbourhood—seemed to be lit up with colourful fairy lights. Red, blue, pink, white, yellow, and green, they twinkled and winked, setting the whole area afire with their diamond brilliance. She put her hands on her cheeks, charmed and speechless.

A pair of arms came around her middle. Ashok drew her back and nuzzled her neck. Annie shivered; she was very sensitive there.

'Hi,' he said softly.

'Hi.' She turned a little in his arms. 'What are those lights?'

Ashok released her and went back towards the bed. He bent to pick up the shirt on the floor and started to put it on. 'It is Diwali. The lights are there to celebrate.' He pulled on his trousers. 'Now, get ready fast. We are going out to celebrate as well.'

Twenty minutes later, they were out on the streets with Ashok's bike. The whole city seemed to have been lit afire;

lights hung from every available corner. All the houses, their balconies, the rooftops—even public buildings and shops and malls—were lit up. People were out on the street, setting off fireworks and crackers. The noises were deafening.

'How do you like it?' Ashok shouted above the din.

'A bit like Christmas, only very noisy!' Annie shouted back.

'Would you like to go back?'

They made their way back after an hour. Annie wanted to have dinner early as she was to start the next leg of her tour the next morning. They were to travel to Rajasthan, the neighbouring state, and the bus would arrive early.

'I suppose I better get back,' Ashok said after dropping her at her hotel.

'But won't you come in? I thought we might have dinner together.' Annie was taken aback.

Ashok shook his head. 'I have to go to a dinner,' he said ruefully. 'My cousin's place. We are to celebrate Diwali together.'

'Of course. Well, I will not make you late then.' Annie tried to smile, but she was afraid it did not come out very well. Ashok noticed it. He lifted his hand and softly cradled her cheek.

'Don't worry. We shall see each other again. I promise you that.'

'Yes, of course. Only, I have a long journey tomorrow, and afterwards . . .'

'Afterwards, when you come back here, I shall see you. I *have* to see you, actually. There can't be any other way,' Ashok said softly. Then he kicked his bike into life and rode off. Annie went in, feeling inexplicably let down. *He is right. He has no commitment to spend his festival with me. He has other friends and family besides me*, she kept telling herself. But it didn't help. *At least he could have kissed me goodnight*, she thought. But she also knew that in India, public display of affection was frowned upon.

As she climbed up the stairs to her room, she felt her eyes dampen. Angrily, she brushed them back, wondering, *What is the matter with me? I am a mature woman, not some silly teenager.*

Later, after she had had her dinner and finished packing, she made a call.

'Annie? Oh my god.'

'Becky.' Annie found herself grinning at the sound of her best friend's voice. She hadn't realized how much she had missed Becky.

'How are you out there, honey?'

'Oh, fabulous.' Annie laughed. 'I feel so happy, Becky. For the first time in months, I feel happy.'

'I am ever so glad to hear that. How is Delhi? And how are the other people on the tour?'

'Delhi is like a fairy land, Becky. There are lights everywhere, and the whole city is celebrating . . .' Annie explained Diwali festivities to Becky. 'And as for friends, well, I have someone . . .'

'Oh?' Becky's antenna sharpened. 'Only one? Who is he? Is he special?'

'What makes you think it is a he?' Annie laughed again.

'Oh, come on! I know I'm right now. Tell me all.'

'Well, I don't know if it is special, but he is very sweet.'

'Sweet? I am not sure I heard right,' Becky teased gently.

'Well, he is extremely good-looking. You remember the hotel I first contacted before I came here?'

'The totally luxurious one? With a spa and gym and a pool and—'

'Yes, yes,' Annie interrupted, laughing. 'Well, Ashok is the assistant manager of one of the many restaurants located in the hotel, and we kept in touch over email.

'Go on.'

'And when I came here, we met, and he has been so sweet. He took me to tour the city, and we spent time exploring and eating street food and—oh, Becky! It's been marvellous!'

'Well, as long as you are sure what you are doing, Annie dear.'

'What do you mean?'

'It seems to me you are almost in love with the guy. Take care of yourself, will you? You are in a foreign country with a man you know little about. I don't want you to get hurt.'

'I am not in love with him. He is a friend—a very kind one—and I will miss him when I leave, but—'

'Well, just take care, will you?'

They talked for a couple of minutes after that. Annie described Diwali to Becky, who thought it was quaint. Then Annie rang off.

As she got ready for bed, she grew thoughtful. Was Becky right? Was she about to fall in love with Ashok?

She lay on the bed and stared at the ceiling for some time before falling into a troubled sleep. Tomorrow would be a long day.

CHAPTER 6

THE NEXT DAY, ANNIE WAS up at the crack of dawn. She had not slept well the night before; her eyelids felt as if they had sand under them, and her head ached. On top of that, the day was foggy, dark, and damp. She wished she could stay in bed, but the bus was to arrive early, and she had to get ready. She splashed cold water on her face to wake herself up properly and then started to get ready.

An hour later, Annie finished breakfast and collected her purse and her luggage, preferring to wait for the bus under the patio. It arrived at eight; she was the last one to be picked up. She found herself a seat towards the back of the bus. It was just as well. She was really not up to making polite conversation with somebody she was only vaguely familiar with. She had hoped to see Ashok right till the moment she boarded the bus, but as they started off, she had to accept that he was not going to show up. 'Oh well,' she sighed. 'Becky was right. He was only being kind to a foreigner in his country after all. Nothing more to it.' She tried to concentrate on the tour operator—what was his name? Nikhil? No, Niraj. He was speaking now.

'We shall be heading towards Jaipur. That is a very old city of Rajasthan. We shall have lunch at a local village on our way. That will also be in Rajasthan. There you can also have a look at how the village people live in India,' Niraj was saying. Annie could feel her eyes close as she listened to his voice wash over her. She had not quite slept the night before, and she was tired. Soon, she was fast asleep, her head resting comfortably on the frame of the window.

When she opened her eyes, the bus had stopped. It was quite late, she deduced, for the sun was high in the sky. She checked her watch; it was past noon.

'Lunch!' Niraj announced. They started to get off the bus. Annie looked around in wonder as she came out. It was quite hot; Delhi seemed pleasanter compared to this heat. There were a few houses clustered together with painted mud walls around them. She guessed they were to have lunch at one of these houses. She took a couple of curious steps forward before spotting an old-fashioned well with wooden frames and a bucket tired with a rope on the side. She eagerly went towards it. There were three young girls at the well, their colourful skirts billowing in the wind. Annie went to them and gestured with her hands and face, trying to convey that she wanted to wash her face. Giggling, the girls dipped the bucket in, drew up half a bucket full of water, and tipped it so that she could wash her face. She cupped her hands and splashed her face with the cool, refreshing water. Soon, there was a queue behind her; the whole bus wanted to have a go. There was much laughing and giggling, but finally, they all trooped inside the village. Inside the wall, there was a courtyard. Annie was surprised to see how clean it was, even if they had to sit down on mats on the dry earth. Girls and women brought out plates laden with food. They were not sure at first, but after the first bite, everyone ate with gusto. For one thing, they were famished after the long drive, and for another, the food was delicious as Annie found to her surprise.

'I have told them to go easy on the chillies, seeing that you all are not used to spicy food,' Niraj said when one of the tourists commented on how delicious the food was. Annie could only be thankful for that piece of thoughtfulness.

Afterwards, they had a turn in the village. They were charmed by the camels tethered in the courtyards of village homes. Annie knew about camels being the prime domestic animal in the deserts, but she was thrilled anyway to see them up close. At one place, they saw women rolling small earthen lamps, and more were put out into the sun to dry. They twinkled in the sun, their bright colours lighting up the arid land. They were for the Diwali celebrations and would be carried to the city markets, Niraj explained. They took leave of the place after a couple of hours.

The next time the bus stopped, it was well past dark. They had arrived at their hotel. Annie peered at the building as they went in, but she could hardly make out anything except brightly lit lamps and a broad driveway. They were tired, so they all had a light dinner and went straight up to bed after that. Annie had to share her room with an elderly lady from their group this time.

The next morning, they all assembled for breakfast in the dining room downstairs before setting out for a tour of the city. As she came down the stairs, her eyes scanned the room of her own volition; she knew he wouldn't be there, of course, but she had to suppress a sigh of disappointment all the same. They gathered around a large table set out under the porch, laden with Indian breakfast, but there was a side table with a toast rack and some cut fruit as well. Annie was relieved as she was not sure about the spicy and fried Indian food. She eagerly went to the small table while most of the others fell upon the table with puri and vegetables with relish. Later, they were served tea in lovely stoneware cups—from the local cottage industry, they were told—before they piled into the bus.

Jaipur was the capital city of Rajasthan, Niraj informed them. It was also known as the Pink City. As their bus drove through the lanes, Annie saw why. The buildings were a distinctive shade of pink.

'Are these pink stones, I wonder?' Annie mused aloud.

'Oh, no, dear.' The lady beside her smiled. She had been Annie's roommate at the hotel. She had a gentle smile and twinkling, kind eyes in a rather faded shade of blue. She had fading blonde hair too, put back in a severe chignon at the back of her neck.

'Not stone. Not all of them anyway,' she continued now. 'It is painted mostly.'

'Oh.' Annie turned back towards the window. It was really colourful outside, with women walking along the sidewalk, their long full skirts billowing in the desert wind. Small children walked to school in neat uniforms, carrying backpacks on their backs. Scooters, cars, and camels vied for spaces in the cramped streets.

'Pink is the colour of hospitality,' Niraj was saying. 'When Queen Victoria and the prince of Wales visited the city in 1876, the king of Jaipur painted the city pink to welcome them. Since then, it has remained so. It became the law. Also, the stones that are used to build houses have a pink hue.'

'Where are we going first?' one of the tourists wanted to know.

'We shall be going to see the Hawa Mahal first,' Niraj replied. 'It means the Palace of Winds.'

'What is that?' Annie asked her companion.

'It is a palace.' She shrugged. Annie laughed. She liked the old lady; she had a friendly face, and last night, they had spent some easy moments together before they had both gone to bed. She was from Australia, Annie knew, and her name was Nancy.

'Well, we shall see when we see it,' Annie said now. 'Personally, I am not much interested in old palaces though.'

'Here we are, ladies and gentlemen, the Hawa Mahal,' Niraj declared.

As they ambled out of the bus, Annie squinted up at the structure before her. At first glance, it seemed like a beehive of a building, high and—as with most of the structures in the city—pink. Then as she got used to the sheer height of the massive stone structure, she became aware of intricate latticework carved out from the pink stone. Each framed a window.

'There are 953 windows in all,' Niraj was saying. 'This latticework was to allow the royal ladies to peek outside and observe the streets below while maintaining their *parda*.'

Annie knew that the royal ladies were not to be seen by people outside the royal family. 'The latticework', Niraj continued, 'also allowed breezes to play inside the palace, creating an air-conditioning effect.'

That was news to the tourists. Murmurs of surprise and admiration went up as they inspected the intricate works on stone, both on the outside and the inside of the Palace of the Winds. From there, they then had a tour of the city palace, at whose edge the Hawa Mahal was located.

About an hour and a half later, Annie stood in front of the Jantar Mantar, the famous observatory. Annie lost interest after some time as she was not overly keen on science, but the huge sundial—the largest in the world, she learned—caught her eye.

'It is amazing, isn't it, how people in the past achieved such great things?' It was Nancy.

'Uh-huh. It is indeed amazing,' Annie agreed.

'I have been to Egypt and Rome, and the ancient monuments never fail to awe me. But India is a different experience altogether,' Nancy shared. 'They are not gigantic structures, true, but their intricacies and wisdom are amazing.'

'I believe it is,' Annie said, 'though this is the first time I am travelling in a foreign country.'

'I believe we shall be off to see the fort of Ajmer next,' Nancy observed before moving away. Sure enough, the bus took them out of the city this time as Ajmer was situated a few kilometres off Jaipur.

Ajmer turned out to be a little town next to Jaipur. The fort was known as Amber Fort, and it lay on the crest of a small hill. The best part of the fort was the mirror hall or the Sheesh Mahal. Annie was wonderstruck at it. Tiny mirrors made up the entire ceiling and also the walls; it was as if millions of diamonds were twinkling, sparkling in the morning light.

'The queen was not allowed to sleep under the sky, but she wanted to see the stars shining,' Niraj was saying. 'So the king ordered the mirror hall to give her an illusion of the open sky. If you light two candles at night, then the reflection turns them into thousands of candles and lights up the entire hall.'

Annie could imagine that. 'It is so beautiful,' she breathed. The walls and the ceiling were covered with exquisitely intricate paintings, all of them adorned with mirror-work. The sheer beauty of it all took her breath away. She suddenly wished Ashok were there with her; she wanted to lie at night and look up at the thousand reflections of the two candles. Almost at once, she felt embarrassed and surreptitiously looked around. *Heavens!* she thought. *I hope nobody has guessed my silly girly thoughts.* But of course, the rest of the tourists were busy with their own admirations, and nobody seemed to have noticed her suddenly flushed face.

Since it was quite late by that time, they decided to have lunch. Niraj had packed food packets, which they had in the cool interiors of the bus. Annie washed down the sandwiches with fruit juice; Niraj arranged all discarded remains neatly in a large plastic bag—which they would later dispose of, he explained solemnly.

Their last stop of the day was the elephant safari. It was located right behind the Ajmer Fort. The large animals seemed friendly enough, and Annie fed them bananas, four each, laughing as they picked them up delicately from her hands. She was not sure about riding them though.

'Come on!' Nancy urged her. 'They are very gentle. And the landscape is beautiful. They say you can see the Aravalli mountain range from here.'

'I don't know. They seem so tall. The ground will be very far away. Don't you think?'

'Come, *memsahib*,' the driver—or the *mahout*—called. 'Laxmi is very gentle.'

'Come on, Annie. See, the seats have railings. You can't possibly fall,' Nancy persuaded. Annie gave in, though not without trepidation. When the elephant heaved to a standing position, she almost screamed, for the seat undiluted crazily, but he held her ground. Finally, the gentle beast began its trek through the arid landscape towards the forested area nearby. Annie was tense for the first few minutes, but gradually, she forgot to be scared as she took in the beautiful landscape around her. The forest was a mystical land— sunlight filtering through branches and leaves, creating fairy dust, and the air laden with the fragrance of wildflowers. Birds chirped, and little monkeys peeped shyly through the bushes. She was sorry to leave the magical land as the elephants started to make their way back to the safari park.

They started their journey back to their hotel after that. It was already dusk as they finally came to a stop at the porch of the hotel. Annie longed for a hot shower. She took the keys from the desk and made her way back to her room. Nancy stayed back for a drink with the others.

CHAPTER 7

As SHE WAS GETTING READY for the shower, Ashok
rang. Her heart skipped as she saw his number on the
screen. She forced herself to sound casual as she answered
the call.

'Hi,' Ashok said softly. 'Where are you?'

'Back at the hotel room,' Annie replied. She was quite
proud of the way her voice remained steady.

'What are you doing?'

'Getting ready to take a shower,' she replied without
thinking.

'Really?' Ashok's voice sharpened naughtily. 'And how
are you getting ready for it?'

'Well . . .' Annie didn't know what to say. For all her
experience in past relationships, she was quite shy when it
came to sexual repartee.

Ashok laughed gently. 'Are you wearing anything?'

'Yes. Yes, I am as a matter of fact. I just came back,
and . . .' Ashok laughed.

'I am sorry, Annie. I just couldn't resist. You are so easy to tease.' His voice grew sober. 'I just wanted to hear your voice.'

'Oh. Well, we visited quite a few places today,' Annie said. Inside she felt elated but nervous. 'We saw the Wind Palace . . .'

'The Wind Palace?'

'Hawa Mahal.'

'Oh, *that* Wind Palace.'

'You are teasing me again,' Annie complained.

'Sorry. I just cannot resist. Go on, please.'

'It was beautiful. And the large sundials. We also went to the Ajmer Fort, and I rode elephants.' Annie knew she was rambling, but she couldn't help it.

'What did you like the best today?'

'The Sheesh Mahal, definitely. It was as if it were lit up with millions of diamonds, you know. And they say that the ceiling looks like a starry night when it is dark.'

'And they are right. I have been there during night-time. It is really an exotic experience.'

'I wished . . .' Annie suddenly bit her lip and stopped herself in time. She was about to blurt out about her fantasy of lying there with Ashok. She blushed furiously and thanked God that there was nobody around to notice her.

'What did you wish, Annie?' Ashok asked softly as if he sensed Annie was about to confide something intimate in him. But she shook her head.

'How was your day?' she asked instead.

'Busy,' Ashok answered easily. 'I had to escort a group of Japanese delegates around the city. They are part of a high-profile meeting with the government.'

'What are you doing now?' Annie could not stop herself from asking.

'Having a slow drink on my balcony before going out to dinner with some friends. And missing you.'

Annie's breath almost stopped; she did not know what to say. Just then the key in the lock turned.

'I have to go now. My roommate is back.' She hung up as Nancy came into the room.

'Have you had your shower? They will be serving dinner in a few minutes.'

'Just going. I will take not more than a couple of minutes.' Annie ducked into the bathroom.

As she stood under the soothing spray of water, Ashok's words came back to her. She could feel her body warm up just by remembering his voice. Ashok spoke softly, but his voice was a deep, husky baritone that managed to bring out goose pimples in her.

'Stop it!' she admonished herself. 'It is no good drooling over a man you barely know.' But she couldn't help remembering what he had said. Did he mean it when he said that he had missed her? Because she missed him. A heck of a lot. As she soaped her body, squeezing body shampoo on to her body, she recalled the feel of his hands when they made love. She yearned for him with a hunger that surprised her.

'Annie?' Nancy was knocking at the door. 'They have served dinner.'

Annie came back with jolt. 'I am almost done, Nancy.' She hastened to wash the soapsuds and quickly dried herself before putting on her clothes. Then she opened the door.

'I am sorry. Am I too late?'

Nancy smiled. 'No, it is all right. I will just have a quick wash, and then we can go downstairs.'

Annie felt awful. Her roommate was such a dear, and now she was probably late because of Annie's stupid middle-aged fantasies. Nancy came out of the bathroom almost as soon as she was in.

'Let's go,' she said before picking up her keys. Together they went down the carved staircase that led to the dining hall, making small talk about the places they had visited that day.

Dinner was a lavish Indian affair. The table was laden with silvery dishes containing sumptuous vegetable curry, chicken, lamb, and Indian flatbread. There was rice pudding and laddu (a round Indian candy) for dessert. They all heaped their plates with food and mingled, chatting about the day while digging into the delicious fare.

Annie felt out of place within so many people; she was still thinking about her conversation with Ashok. She didn't want to read too much into what he had said, but she couldn't help turning what he had said over and over in her head and feel a shiver of thrill deep inside. Did he really miss her?

'Hi,' a deep voice said at her shoulder. Startled, she looked back and saw a tall man smiling down at her. He looked to be in his late forties and was casually dressed in jeans and an open-necked T-shirt. Annie smiled back; she liked the way his eyes crinkled at the corners when he smiled.

'Hi,' she replied.

'I am Greg, from UK,' he said, offering his hand.

'Annie,' she replied, shaking his hand. He had a firm grip, she noticed, not unpleasant at all. 'From USA, Florida.'

'Right. I noticed you the very first day. How are you holding up here? I must say I find this all a bit too overwhelming.'

'Oh. I love this. The weather, the food, the landscapes,' Annie said sincerely. It was true. So far, she had liked whatever she had come across, a charming hotel assistant manager included.

'Don't you find it appalling? The heat, the flies, the poverty?' Greg raised his brows. 'Interesting.'

Annie suddenly wanted to get away from him, but she couldn't think of a way without appearing rude. 'I have really not noticed them,' she said civilly but with considerable coolness. 'I mean, of course they are there, but there are also these wonderful people who are so hospitable, the colours, the food . . . don't you think?' she asked.

'Hmm.' Greg shrugged. 'I personally can't wait to get back home.'

'Annie!' Nancy beckoned her. 'Come over here and taste this beautiful dessert.'

Annie moved over to the table gladly. 'I am not sure I should have dessert.' She laughed but helped herself to a spoonful of the wonderful rice pudding.

'Come on. You have a wonderful figure,' Nancy said, her eyes twinkling. 'You don't have to worry about weight.'

'My metabolism is not what it used to be, you know.'

'None of ours are, dear. But that is no reason to stop living, is it?' Nancy helped herself to some more of the sweet pudding.

Niraj ambled over to them. 'How is the food, ma'am? Everything good?' he wanted to know.

'Everything is fine,' Nancy replied.

'Where are we going tomorrow?' Annie asked.

'Well, we are to visit the block printing factory, and then we shall go to the bird sanctuary at Bharatpur.'

'Block printing?' Annie wanted to know.

'They make all kinds of clothes, saris, scarves, even bed sheets and the like,' Niraj explained.

'That will be fun!' Nancy was excited.

'Yes, but I am not sure about the birds,' Annie replied. She put down her plate on the side table. 'I think I shall turn in.'

'Oh, but there are drinks and music after dinner,' Niraj said. 'Won't you stay for that?'

Annie shook her head. 'When do we start tomorrow?'

'After breakfast. About nine.'

'I shall have to do some packing also, so I have to be up early. I will bid you all goodnight.' She smiled before making her way back towards the stairs.

Once she was back in her room, Annie felt strangely depressed. She could hear laughter and music from below; she regretted being on her own, but it was too late now to go back. She sighed and started to put her things into her case; they would be moving out of the hotel the next day. Afterwards, she cleaned her teeth and brushed her hair before getting into bed. She wanted to fall asleep right then, but to her vexation, it was a long time coming. She felt too restless to read a book, and the sounds of revelry downstairs would have interfered anyway. Maybe she could put on some clothes and join the fun. Wasn't that the point of this tour? To have fun? But she also knew that once she went down, she would want to leave the crowd again. It was not them; it was her. She felt unsettled after Ashok's call. She wanted to be with him instead of a bus full of strangers, but she was scared stiff of what would follow after she saw him again. She resolved to be aloof and cool if he called her again, and she turned over, plumping the pillows before willing herself to sleep. By the time Nancy came into their room, swaying slightly, she was fast asleep.

CHAPTER 8

A MIDDLE-AGED MAN GREETED THE PARTY with folded hands at the entrance of the block printing company. They were escorted to the cool interior of the office, which was a small room at the front of a moderate building really, with a few chairs and a big swing chair on the veranda. They were offered *chas*, a milky drink made out of sour curd. Annie was not sure of it at first, but it proved to be quite refreshing after the first tentative sip.

'We are so honoured to have you today,' the man was saying. 'The workers will be very inspired by your visit.'

He was the manager of the factory, apparently. 'Where is the owner?' Annie wondered aloud.

'Oh, *memsaab*, our owner does not stay here. She stays in Delhi and comes here often—sometimes more than once a month,' the manager, Mr Meena, replied.

'The owner is a woman? Remarkable.' It was Greg. Annie felt a bit annoyed by the touch of patronization in his tone.

'And why do you think that is remarkable?' she challenged Greg softly.

Greg shrugged. 'Indian women . . .' he began before Annie stopped him with 'Are very capable, thank you.'

'Now, are we ready to have a look at the factory?' Niraj intervened hastily, seeing the light of battle in Annie's eyes.

They all ambled out of the office after that.

The factory was very hot. After the coolness of the office, it was a shock to experience that heat. About twenty-five people, men and women, worked under the shed. They were shown how wooden blocks were diced into patterns and then stamped with colours on the clothes, where the pattern took shape. They were working both on silk and cotton. Different fabrics were for different uses, Mr Meena explained. There were bed linens, scarves, saris, dress materials, and even small napkins and tableware. All the colours used were vegetable dyes, derived from natural resources, they were told. They came back to the office after the tour; Annie was charmed by the radiant smiles on the women's faces. They looked rustic and weather-beaten, but they had a very direct, bold gaze that spoke of resolve and determination. She suspected they were fiercely independent in spite of their poverty. She also loved their colourful skirts and heavy jewellery.

Mr Meena was showing them the stock of products piled inside a room beside the office. Most of them bought items from the stock. Nancy bought a brightly coloured scarf and a long *kurta*, a knee-length top with long sleeves. Annie bought a green-and-red scarf, several napkins, tableware in bright hues (for herself and to take back to Becky), and a long ankle-length dress in a dazzling shade of flame and yellow. They then thanked the manager and went on their way.

By the time they reached Bharatpur, it was well past noon. The sky was dazzling, and the heat stifling. The sanctuary actually housed more animals than birds, Annie thought. There were deer with big antlers, and she heard that there were leopards. It was a national park and was covered with beautiful trees, shrubs, and a big lake. The tourists were thrilled when they spotted some sambar deer and started to take photographs. Annie felt her phone vibrate. She took it out—they all had turned their phones to silent mode—and saw that it was Ashok. She gazed at the number, not knowing what to do. She could not take the call. Did she even want to? The phone fell silent after some time. Annie was not sure how she felt. On the one hand, she was relieved that the decision was taken out of her hands. On the other, she felt a deep regret at missing this chance to hear his voice. They moved on, and after some time when the tour came to an end, they boarded the bus. After some time though, the bus stopped. At first glance, they could not see anything interesting.

'What are we doing here, mate?' an Australian man called out from the back of the bus.

'We shall see a stepwell here,' Niraj replied.

'What?'

'Stepwell. It is a type of water reservoir unique to this part of India. Please follow me, and you shall see what I mean.' Niraj climbed down from the bus, and they all followed, puzzled and a little intrigued.

The stepwell had steps built into the sides so that people could reach the bottom of the well. It was much larger than a common well, and the stairs seemed to be carved out geometrically, making it a complex structure. As they went down, they saw people sitting on the steps in the cooling afternoon breeze—middle-aged ladies, small children with their nannies, young couples, even old men and women. As they climbed down, Niraj said, 'These wells made sure that the ancient Rajput had a supply of water at any time of the year. This is arid desert area, you know.'

'We know,' Nancy said in her driest voice, but her eyes twinkled. Niraj laughed.

'Yes, ma'am, I know. I mean, I know you know. Also, in those days, the people of the town used to gather around here. The bottom part is much cooler than the top, you see.'

Annie and the others could see that. In spite of the desert sun, it was surprisingly pleasant as they went down. 'Even the royals used to spend time here during summer. This is the royal chamber,' Niraj declared. They were inside a room with intricate stone carvings and even a stage, which Niraj said was for the performing arts.

Annie thought it was brilliant. She turned to Greg. 'What do you think?'

Even Greg was impressed. 'It is wonderful—very innovative. They had their own air-conditioning system in place everywhere, it seems.'

Annie thought about the Hawa Mahal and was inclined to agree. They all spent a few minutes in the cool interiors of the well before making their way back up.

The bus started towards Fatehpur Sikri, an abandoned city by the Moghals. Annie's phone rang just as the bus took to the highway. It was Ashok again. This time she took the call.

'I called you before, but you didn't take it' was the first thing Ashok said.

'I am sorry. I was not supposed to take a call. The phone was in silent mode. We are at the sanctuary,' Annie said.

Then she added, 'I also had not checked my phone since then.'

'Hmm. How is your trip going?'

'I am liking it very much. We were just at a well where you can go down the steps, and it is much cooler at the bottom.'

'Of course it is. When can I see you, do you think?'

'I am not sure,' Annie said cautiously. She didn't want to give the impression that she was easy. 'We shall go to Agra next, and then I don't know what they have in mind.'

'I want you to view Taj Mahal with me—the first time anyway.'

'Why?'

'Why? It is the most romantic place under the sun. That is why,' Ashok said.

'I would rather see it with the rest of my fellows, thank you.' Annie felt a twinge of unease. She was not sure what Ashok wanted of her. And she thought he was definitely taking it too fast. She wasn't ready for this. Not yet.

'Okay,' Ashok said easily; he did not seem to be feeling any loss at her refusal, Annie thought, feeling perversely peeved. 'When are you going to be back here though?'

'Maybe in a day or two.' Annie did not want him to be too sure of her.

'I miss you, Annie,' Ashok said softly, sending goosebumps through her spine. 'I want you in my arms now.'

'Well, you can't.' Panic made Annie curt. 'I am in a bus in Rajasthan, and you are in Delhi.'

'I know. That is why I can't wait for you to be here. Do you remember how we felt together?'

'That was a one-time thing. I do not intend to repeat it,' Annie said primly.

'Don't you? Come here soon. Don't be late, Annie.' Ashok rung off.

Annie gazed at the handset in her hands, dazed by it all, before putting it back in her purse. 'Trouble in paradise?' Nancy said in a low voice.

'What? Oh, no. No, nothing like that.' Annie gave a little laugh, but it came across as forced and unnatural. Nancy was not fooled, but she wisely held her words.

When they reached Fatehpur Sikri, it was almost time for the sun to set. Annie wasn't sure they would get enough time to see anything significant, but Niraj said watching the sun go down over the ruins of the city was a sight not to be missed. They went to see the great mosque, which was said to be an exact replica of the main mosque at Mecca. Later they continued to Agra, where the grand viewing of the Taj Mahal was scheduled for the next day.

CHAPTER 9

Taj Mahal seemed elusive at first. All they could see was a dingy lane filled up with dirt, numerous stalls, rickshaws, people on bicycles, even a giant bull that refused to budge or make way for the column of tourists cautiously continuing their journey.

'This is terrible!' Annie had a kerchief firmly pressed on her nostrils. 'I am sure we are at the wrong place.'

'Not the wrong place, ma'am. This is the right place. You will see.' Niraj had heard her.

They went through a narrow gateway made of red stone, and then they all stood still.

Before them was a vision of sheer grandeur and loveliness they had never encountered before. Even Nancy, a seasoned traveller of exotic places all over the world, was awestruck. Built entirely of white marble, the seventh wonder of the world seemed to float on air before their dazzled eyes.

'Oh my god!' she said softly under her breath.

'Come on, let's go forward,' Greg said.

'Before we proceed, ladies and gentlemen, I wish to inform you of something.' It was Niraj. 'This is the wonder of Taj Mahal. This gate is a special gate. If you look through the gateway, the Taj Mahal will appear smaller to you. But if you walk backward, keeping your eye on the Taj Mahal, it will seem bigger.'

'My god, it is true!' Annie breathed. And it was. As soon as they started to move backward, the snowy structure seemed to get bigger, but the moment they started towards it, it got smaller.

'It is an optical illusion,' Greg declared, 'but very cleverly done.'

The marble mausoleum was surrounded by beautifully crafted gardens, and they had to remove their shoes. The guide started to tell them about the history and intricacies of the structure. Annie looked up at the sky. It was brilliant blue, and the Taj Mahal seemed dazzling under the bright sun. Her thoughts went back to Ashok. He had wanted to be there when she saw it the first time. She wished she had him—somebody—with her at that moment.

'Fascinating, don't you think?' a familiar baritone said softly at her shoulder. Startled out of her skin, she turned swiftly to see Ashok looking down at her, a quizzical glint in his eyes.

'You! What are you doing here?' she gasped.

'The same as you. Looking and marvelling at the most romantic homage of the world.'

Annie darted a quick look over her shoulders. Her companions had vanished—most probably taking a tour of the inner chambers. She turned back towards Ashok, drinking in the sight of him. He looked simply ravishing in a pair of blue denims and a light-blue shirt, open at the neck, with the sleeves turned back to reveal his forearms. His blue-black hair played softly in the breeze.

'I know that,' she said severely. 'You knew I am with my tour company.'

'Yes,' he agreed unabashedly. 'I also knew that you wanted me to be here.'

'You wish!' Annie scoffed even if her heart sang. 'Don't you have anything better to do?'

'Today is my off day. But even if it were not, I would have come. Now, are you going to stand here all day and pretend that you aren't glad that I am here, or are we going to have a tour of the place? Just you and me.'

'I would rather view it from here, thank you,' Annie said primly, choosing to ignore the rest of his words.

They sat on the parapet of the Taj. Annie gazed at the intricate floral designs on the walls; the minarets seemed to stretch out towards the sky from her angle.

'This is the best homage a man can pay to a woman,' she sighed.

'Hmm.' Ashok leaned back on his palms, looking up at the elegant Persian dome. 'Do you know she died at childbirth?'

'So? It was quite common on those days. Prenatal care was not so strong, you know.'

'She bore fourteen children.'

'That only proves that they were very much in love.'

'Really?' Ashok's voice grew low. 'You think they made love often?'

Annie blushed in a deep red; she quickly averted her head. 'Let's go and sit there. The benches are cool.' Ashok took pity on her.

The benches were indeed cool, placed under the shady trees. From there, they could view the Taj at a distance. For some time, they sat in companionable silence, admiring its sheer beauty before Ashok spoke.

'What are you doing after this?'

'Oh. I really am not sure. Niraj was saying something about the Agra Fort.'

'Of course. And later?'

'We shall check into our hotel and have dinner, I suppose.'

'Have dinner with me tonight.'

'With you? I am not sure that is a good idea.'

'Why not?' Ashok challenged.

'Um . . . because . . .' She was suddenly at a loss for words.

'See? There is no reason why we should not have dinner together.'

'Only dinner. Nothing else,' Annie said in her best stern voice.

'What else?' Ashok raised his eyebrows. 'We shall spend some time together, hopefully enjoy the food. That is if that is all that you are expecting.'

'I am. What do you think I am?' Annie snapped.

'A beautiful woman who is totally unaware of her charms,' Ashok replied promptly. Then before Annie could say anything, he stood up and said, 'I shall have to leave now. Your companions are back anyway.'

'I thought you said you had the day off,' Annie said peevishly. The fact was she did not want him to leave.

Ashok laughed. 'I do. But I have to get ready for dinner.' He suddenly bent and kissed her fully on the mouth. Straightening up, he lifted his hand in farewell and was gone. Annie felt like stomping her feet. He made her so mad!

'Annie! There you are. Niraj was worrying that you might be lost,' Nancy called out.

Annie got up from the bench and went towards the party. 'I was not lost. I just did not want to go inside. It is much more beautiful from here.'

They went to see the Agra Fort after that. Made out of red stone, it was a majestic structure like the other historical sites in India. They checked into their hotel after that; it was a new hotel this time. It was located centrally, which was an advantage. Nancy and Annie decided to share again; they had gotten used to each other. Annie liked Nancy; she was cheerful and a good company even if she did not speak much. Annie preferred it that way. They put away their cases and freshened up before going down for drinks.

A few of the others from their party were already at the lobby. Annie ordered a cocktail while Nancy accepted a gin and tonic before they joined the others.

'Who was he?'

Annie turned. A young woman lounged across from her; she crossed her shapely legs and smiled lazily at Annie. 'Hi. I am Pat.'

'I am Annie.' Annie took the slim manicured hand offered to her briefly before turning to her drink.

'Who was he then?'

Annie eyed her thoughtfully. Pat was in her late twenties, with reddish-blonde hair that glowed like burnished gold in the soft light of the lobby. She was also slim and, from what Annie could make out, had legs that went on forever. She hated her on sight.

'I am not sure what you mean.'

'The hunk at the Taj. Is he your friend?'

'Oh. Uh, yes. Yes, of course. A friend.'

'Known him long?' Pat took a sip of her drink.

'Actually, yes. I know him from before this trip.' Annie sipped her drink as well, enjoying the coolness against her throat; she had not realized that she was so parched.

'Excuse me. I have to get ready for dinner.' Annie put down her glass and got up from the sofa.

'Annie!' Nancy called her from the bar. Annie went to her, glad to be away from Pat. 'Niraj says there is a great nightclub nearby. Fancy a trip? After dinner. We are going.'

Annie shook her head. 'I am going out for dinner. Later sometime. You go and have a good time.'

'Okay. See you later.' Nancy smiled.

CHAPTER 10

ANNIE WENT UP THE STAIRS, grateful that Nancy did not pry. She went inside her room and opened her case. She felt unsure but excited about the dinner. Now she eyed the dresses spread on the bed, unable to make up her mind. Would she go for formal or semiformal? Or would casual be the sensible option? She wished she knew what to expect from Ashok. Was he simply being friendly or . . .

Her eyes went back to the bed. She picked up a blue blouse with a lace collar, grimaced, and then threw it. She detested it. For the life of her, she could not even remember where she had bought it, let alone why she had bought it.

Maybe she would call him and cancel dinner? Then she saw it.

It was an ankle-length chiffon dress, cream coloured, with a gathered bodice and halter neck. The straps were dull gold, leaving her shoulders and arms bare, which shone bronze against the cream. The dress fell in soft swirls against her legs and made her feel feminine and elegant. She let her hair fall down her back in naturally graceful curls and touched up her cheeks and lips with coral. Putting her feet into strappy, low-heeled sandals, she sprayed herself with her favourite perfume and picked up her purse before going out of the room. She wanted to wait for him in the lobby downstairs; she didn't trust herself with him in the same room.

Nancy and the others were chatting when she emerged in the lobby. Greg raised a hand when she saw her, and she smiled a greeting to him. Nancy turned to see and lifted a brow, but she said nothing. Annie was glad; she felt self-conscious as it was.

'Wow! All dressed up. Going somewhere?' It was Pat, the young girl who had earlier asked about Ashok.

'As a matter of fact, yes.' Annie did not elaborate. They would know when Ashok came to pick her up anyway. And sure enough, he appeared at the door at that precise moment. He was dressed more formally than usual, wearing dark trousers and a midnight-blue shirt. Annie thought he looked very chic.

He smiled at her and began to make his way towards her; Annie was glad to notice that he did not glance anywhere else once he located her.

'I am not late, am I? I hope I have not kept you waiting,' he said as he came near her.

'No. I just came down,' Annie said.

'Good. Let's go then.'

They left the foyer, and Ashok asked the valet to bring around his car.

Annie was relieved once they were out of the interested glances.

The car arrived. It was a black sedan of a make that Annie did not recognize. Today Ashok decided to use his car because he knew he would have no problem in finding parking as he was taking Annie to his home unknown to her.

She got into it. Ashok closed the door of the passenger side before walking around to the driver's side and getting in.

As he pulled out into the main street, Annie asked, 'Where are we going?'

'To have dinner.'

'I know that, silly. I meant the venue. Is it very far from here?'

'We shall see.'

There was silence in the car for a few minutes as Ashok concentrated on driving, and Annie observed the scenery outside. She never ceased to wonder how close the cars would come to one another, yet they always managed to pull back in the nick of time. She mentioned it to Ashok.

'You know, I marvel at how close the cars veer towards one another. Sometimes I close my eyes in fright. Yet they never touch.'

'We are used to it,' Ashok said lightly.

'Yes, I understand that. But back home, if this happened, I am sure there would be a huge pile-up.'

They turned into a smaller street, and after a few minutes, Ashok stopped the car. Annie looked around in surprise. It seemed like a residential area, and she couldn't locate any restaurant or a hotel. She looked at Ashok in surprise.

'Where are we?'

Ashok got out of the car and walked to Annie's side of the car. He opened the door and said with a flourish, 'To my humble abode, madam. Please come in and make me honoured.'

'Your—this is your home?' Annie gasped. She hadn't imagined he would do this. But she felt she had little choice even though she was uneasy about it. She got out of the car, albeit a bit reluctantly.

'I wish you had told me before,' she said as she followed him up the short path to the lobby of the multi-storeyed building Ashok led her to.

'Why? Would that have made any difference?'

Annie looked at him helplessly. Ashok sighed as he pressed the button for the elevator. 'Relax, Annie. Nothing will happen that you don't want to. I am looking forward to having a meal with you in peace and quiet, where we enjoy each other's company.'

Annie said nothing as they rode up in silence. They came up to his floor, and Ashok took the key out of his pocket.

'If it makes you too uneasy, I can take you back downstairs, and we shall have dinner at a restaurant.'

'No, no this is fine. I am just—it's okay.' Annie was determined not to be a spoilsport.

'Good.' Ashok turned the key in the lock. Annie went in, feeling much like the proverbial lamb at the slaughter.

The living room was spacious, with a large window overlooking the dining area. The sitting area was done up in shades of white and light green, with pristine white faux marble floors, giving the area a cool, refreshed look. A large cream sofa dominated the area, with tiny cushions in pastel colours dotting the back. The curtains were of green and cream cotton, and there were a few chairs as well as a couple of ottomans. A few framed pictures from Indian artists completed the look.

'This is very tastefully done,' Annie remarked as she looked around.

'You like it? I am glad. A friend of mine helped me do it up. She is an interior designer,' Ashok said as he switched on the overhead chandelier.

A female friend? Are they more than friends? Annie instantly wondered and then shook her head at her silly thoughts. What did it matter to her if they were more than friends or not? Just because they had made love once did not mean that she had any rights over him. None at all, in fact.

'Annie? Annie. Are you okay?' Ashok was asking. Annie realized she was standing frozen in the middle of the room and hastily moved over to one of the overstuffed chairs. Sinking on it, she smiled up at him.

'I am okay. So what are we having? Do you cook?'

Ashok shook his head laughingly. 'I am hopeless at cooking. I have had dinner brought in from a local restaurant. All we have to do is warm it up.'

'Shall I help?' Annie made to get up from her chair, but Ashok shook his head again.

'You are a guest. Just sit back and relax. I shall do it all. Would you like to have a drink? I have red and white wine and some juice, I think.'

'Juice would be fine, thank you.' Annie thought she needed a clear head for the night ahead.

As she sipped her juice, Ashok turned on the microwave and started heating dinner. They made small talk as he laid out the table expertly; he was in the hospitality business after all. At last, everything was on the table, and he turned out the overhead light. An oversized counter lamp provided light on the table, surrounding the table and the chairs in an intimate glow while the rest of the living area remained dark.

Annie eyed the bright food with a little trepidation. Even after her Indian tour, she was not always sure of the cuisine.

'These are not too hot, are they? I am not sure about having chillies,' she said.

'Not too spicy at all,' Ashok reassured her. 'I know you don't like hot food, and I ordered accordingly. I think you will like it.'

And she did. After the first tentative bite, she started with more gusto and thoroughly enjoyed the lovely yellow lentil soup and curried lamb with Indian flatbread. There was also fish grilled in a clay oven. Ashok said it was a Punjabi delicacy, from where he belonged. As they ate, he talked about his job and asked about hers. He wanted to go abroad but had no opportunity till date. He had never been out of India, as a matter of fact.

'Have you travelled a lot?' he asked her.

'Not really. I am from Guyana. You see, my mother was Dutch, and she was born in Surinam. She met and married my father and made her life in Guyana. She was a nurse.'

'Was?'

Annie shrugged. 'She has passed on. They both are.'

'So you grew up in Guyana?'

'Went to school, got married, got divorced, moved to Miami, got married and divorced again, and here I am. That's pretty much it.'

'Hmmm. Tell me about your childhood.' Ashok put a piece of cauliflower in his mouth and chewed thoughtfully. Annie wished he wouldn't do that; the movement of his lips as he chewed brought back memories of his kisses.

'Annie?'

'What? Oh, sorry. There is not much to say, really. My father was an accountant. My mother was a nurse. They settled in Guyana before I was born. But I have not been there for a long time now—almost thirty years. And after my gran died, I lost touch with the rest of them as well.'

'My family is from Punjab. But you know that already.'

'Hmm. Yes, of course. But what about the rest of your family?'

'My parents are in Punjab, and my older brother is working in the corporate sector. He is settled in Mumbai.'

'Okay. Have you been to Mumbai?'

'Of course. But with my kind of job, there is not much scope to take holidays, so I spend most of my days here. I am taking time off because you are here now. I have accumulated some leave, so I figured why not spend it in the pleasure of your company?'

They had finished eating. Ashok got up from the table and began to clear the dirty dishes. He piled them in the sink in the kitchen and came back where Annie was still seated at the table, wiping his hands.

'Coffee?' he asked. Annie looked up. He had rolled back his sleeves, and the towel was tucked at his waist. His hair was a bit rumpled, and his face was flushed from the heat in the kitchen, or so Annie assumed. Somehow, it all seemed a bit too intimate, this domestic setting. She suddenly felt it difficult to breathe.

'Annie? Would you like coffee?'

'Thank you. But I must insist on making it this time,' Annie said in a firm voice.

'Okay,' Ashok laughingly agreed. 'You will find mugs on the counter and sugar and coffee in the top right-hand cupboard.'

'Right.' Annie went to the kitchen and filled up the bright red kettle from the tap before putting it on the stove. She opened the cupboard, and sure enough, there was sugar and instant coffee in glass jars stacked neatly along with other supplies. She picked up two coffee mugs from the counter in a pattern of red-and-blue checks and set about making the beverage.

When she came back to the living room, Ashok was settled comfortably on the sofa. He had kicked off his shoes and was now barefoot. Annie set the tray down on the low table and made to move away, but Ashok took her wrist in a light grip and tugged. She sat down on the sofa in a heap. Ashok leaned over and picked up one mug. Taking a sip, he sighed in appreciation before putting it down on the floor beside him. Annie took up her mug and sipped it as well. They sat there in comfortable silence for a few minutes, simply sipping their coffees and contemplating their own thoughts. Annie felt strangely at peace; it was as if being near him brought her a sense of fulfilment as never before. Vaguely she wondered at it and then decided to think later and enjoy the moment for now.

Annie put down her empty mug on the table and turned towards Ashok. He was gazing at her, very still, his eyes half-closed. For some reason, she felt self-conscious.

'I suppose I'd better make a move,' she said, her voice shaking just a little bit. 'The others will be wondering . . .'

Ashok leaned over and kissed her hard on the lips before she could finish her words. Annie gasped. Ashok pushed one hand through her hair, holding the nape of her neck in a firm grasp as he deepened the kiss. His other hand went around her waist until she was flush up against him. They fell on the sofa.

After a few minutes, Ashok lifted his head. 'Not here,' he murmured. Taking Annie by her hand, he went through a door to the left of the living room.

Once inside, they discarded their clothes in a hurry. Annie just had time to register the king-sized bed in the middle of the room before he went down on the soft mattress with her. She could feel the coolness of the soft sheets behind her back, which contrasted with the hard heat of his body on top of hers. Her last rational thought was she would be really late at the hotel before she gave herself to the sensations assailing all her senses.

CHAPTER 11

'ANNIE. ANNIE?'
Annie did not want to come out of her sleepy haze in a hurry; she flicked at the hand that brushed her face.

'Annie? Wake up, honey.' Ashok gently tucked a swath of dark-honey hair behind her ear. 'You have to get back to the hotel. They will be wondering.'

'What?' mumbled Annie. She turned over and stretched. Her muscles felt sore but pleasantly so. She blinked her eyes open. 'Who will wonder?'

'Your tour mates, for one thing.' Ashok smiled down at her. He was dressed in a round-necked T-shirt and . . . Annie sat up in a hurry.

'You are dressed?' she said. It all came back to her in a rush. They had dinner at his place, and then—she felt herself blushing right down to her toes. Ashok noticed it as well and laughed.

'Come on now! You are not feeling shy, are you? Imagine that!' He raised one eyebrow mockingly.

'And why not?' Annie exclaimed angrily, gathering up the light blanket firmly around her. She suddenly felt acutely self-conscious of her nakedness, and that did not improve her mood at all. At that moment, she felt like punching him under the eye—and not gently either. How dare he laugh at her?

'Relax,' Ashok said gently, sobering up as he saw the light of battle in Annie's eyes. 'I was not laughing at you, you know. It's just that you are so delightful, I can't help myself sometimes.' He sat down on the side of the bed; Annie could feel the mattress dip with his weight. Somehow that felt a lot more intimate than the actual act of lovemaking, though she knew not why. She felt herself relax a little.

'I do have to get back. They will wonder about me, you are right.' But she still could not bring herself to let go of the blanket and dress herself.

'I am too gauche,' she berated herself silently. But Ashok seemed to understand. He stood up.

'I shall make some coffee before you go,' he said and left the room. The moment he left, Annie scooted over to where her clothes lay in rumpled disarray on a chair at the corner. She quickly pulled them on and then hastily pulled a brush through her hair. There was nothing she could do about her make-up, so she left it at that. She wished she could find a mirror though; she hoped her eye make-up hadn't run. But the room was way too masculine to have a vanity or a mirror. She felt a pang of envy as she remembered his woman friend who had decorated the flat for him.

Ashok looked up from where he was pouring out coffee at the breakfast counter as she emerged from the bedroom. Seeing her hover uncertainly at the door, he put down the pot and came forward, drawing her in his arms without a word. For long moments, they just stood there, Annie gathered in his arms, not speaking at all. The silence was enhanced by the steady tick-tock of a clock somewhere in the living room. Eventually, Ashok sighed—the sound long and soft—before nuzzling the top of her head very gently. Annie felt tears gather up in her eyes; it was as if he knew the exact state of her emotions without the need for any spoken word. She had never found anyone in her life till now who could understand her senses so well, and she would have to leave him once she flew home. The thought brought pain like she had never encountered before—not even when Zack had told her that he was leaving her for another woman. It was nothing compared to this. She felt as if a sharp weapon were slashing her insides; she actually felt the physical pain. Tears streamed out of the corners of her eyes and fell unchecked on her cheeks.

Ashok tipped her face to him slowly and brushed the tears with his fingers. The gentleness of his gesture broke her heart.

'I wish . . .' he said helplessly.

Annie nodded. 'I know,' she said. It was true. She knew what he wanted to say. She felt it too. 'But I have to go.' She sighed and looked up at him, firming her quivering chin resolutely. 'Will you please drop me back to my hotel?'

'Of course.' Without a word, Ashok released her and went to retrieve the keys from the coffee table at the centre of the living room. Annie slung her purse on her shoulder, and they proceeded down on the elevator. There was complete silence as they descended; neither felt inclined to talk. Something had shifted in their easy friendship. Both acknowledged it but felt unsure about how to deal with it.

Ashok seated Annie before walking around and getting behind the wheel of his car. They cruised down the almost deserted streets of the city. Only a few cars whizzed past at this late hour. Annie gazed out at the dark night, a thousand thoughts in her mind. Her flight was the next day—night actually. She had to pack . . . There were calls to be made and—

Suddenly Ashok braked hard. The car stopped with a jolt as Annie was shocked out of her reverie.

'For God's sake,' he swore under his breath. Before Annie could comprehend what was going on, he turned the car and was speeding back the way they had come.

'What are you doing?' Annie said.

'What does it look like I am doing? We are going back,' Ashok said through his teeth.

'But why? I have to go back.'

'Shut up and let me drive.' Ashok snapped his eyes on the road. Annie glanced at him nervously. His lips were drawn in a grim line, his face stonily determined. Her eyes fell on his hands. His long tapered fingers tightly gripped the steering wheel, the knuckles showing white with strain. She lapsed into silence.

They came to a halt at his apartment block. Ashok got out of the car, came round to her side, yanked the door, and hauled her out before marching towards the elevator.

'Now, wait a minute!' Annie gasped. 'If you think—'

'We shall talk once we go up.' Ashok gave her a look that warned her that he was at the end of his control. She fell silent again.

Once inside the flat, Ashok let go of her hand and sighed. He raked his hands through his hair, which stood up on end, giving him a sweetly endearing look, rather like a small boy, Annie thought. He looked back at Annie, who stood hovering near the door, unsure of what to expect next.

'I am sorry,' Ashok said gently. 'But we cannot part this way, don't you see?'

Annie's eyes fell. 'But what other way is there?'

'I don't know. I really don't. All I know is that this is the wrong way. I just don't—I don't know what the right way is,' Ashok said in a low voice.

'My flight leaves tomorrow, Ashok. I have to go back home.'

'Yes, of course. I see that.' He took a step towards her and then stopped in the middle of the room. 'At least let's have this day. We can have this single day, don't you see?' He lifted tortured eyes towards her; Annie had no resistance to his pleading gaze. She let her purse fall on the ground with a thud and flew into his arms. Ashok held her in a hug so close that she felt breathless.

They stood like that, for how long she had no idea, rocking on their heels. Eventually, he lifted his head and began to kiss her. At first, they rained on her face softly like warm drops, but soon they gathered force till he was ardently pressing his mouth on hers. Her lips opened of her own volition, and her arms went around his neck, her fingers digging into the hair at the nape of his neck. Ashok's arms were wrapped around her closely, one around her back and the other around her hips, almost half-lifting her off the ground. He moved his face this way and that till he had fused his mouth to hers to his satisfaction. Somehow, they moved towards the bedroom, holding each other, and found themselves on the bed as they made love passionately, and no one or nothing else mattered at that moment.

A long time afterwards, Annie stirred. She moved her arm languidly, her body pleasantly sluggish. Her fingers played softly over his skin, skimming his back and shoulders. 'They will wonder,' she said in a low voice.

Ashok did not move. But he lifted a hand, which he then let fall heavily beside her head on the pillow. 'Hmmm.'

Annie laughed. 'You purred.'

'Did I?' He opened one eye and then slowly closed it again.

'Yes, you did, you big cat,' she teased. 'Definitely a purr.'

'I am a tiger,' Ashok drawled, his mouth widening in a satisfied grin.

Annie hit his shoulders gently with the palm of her hand. 'I have to call Nancy first thing in the morning, or she will worry. She is such a dear,' she said, yawning as she rolled over and settled herself beneath Ashok's arms as she closed her eyes and fell asleep.

CHAPTER 12

THEY SPENT THE BETTER PART of the morning in bed, making love and talking. Annie found herself giggling like a schoolgirl as Ashok tickled her ribs softly. They lay in bed in content dishevelment, and he softly drew a lock of her hair down her bare breasts.

'That tickles! Stop it!' Annie laughed in protest, but he continued to find pleasure in tickling Annie. Just then, her cell phone trilled. It was Nancy. Annie made a rueful face at Ashok as she saw who was calling.

'Annie?' Nancy sounded calm. 'Where are you?'

'Umm, with a friend, Nancy. I am sorry. I should have let you know, but . . .'

'Friend? The young handsome guy friend of yours?'

'Uh-huh.'

'Are you okay, honey?'

'More than okay, Nancy. I shall see you when we leave for the airport.'

'Oh, but we are having a picnic, all of us, today. Won't you join us?'

'I shall see you later. Have fun. Bye.'

'Bye, Annie.'

Ashok took the phone from her hand and laid it down with neat precision on the bedside table. Then he sat up and swung his legs on the floor.

'Where are you going?' Annie felt a momentary pang of panic and then immediately chastised herself for it.

'To get some coffee. I need the stamina, madam.' He bent down and picked up his shorts. Pulling them on, he winked down at her before strolling out of the bedroom.

Annie stifled a sigh of disappointment before she gathered her clothes and went to the bathroom. She found a set of new toothbrushes in the cabinet beside the mirror. She borrowed one without asking Ashok and brushed her teeth. As she looked in the mirror, she grimaced. Her hair was a mess; it needed a good wash before she boarded the plane tonight. The thought of leaving brought a sharp pain in her gut; she almost doubled over. Then she squared her shoulders stoically and headed for the shower.

There was bath soap and shampoo, but they were all for males. Well, she had to make do. She stepped into the warm spray of water. Pouring out a dollop of shampoo, she set about lathering her hair.

The curtain was shoved aside, and then a pair of male hands set about massaging her scalp. She almost screamed before she knew that Ashok had stepped into the shower with her. The sight and touch of his magnificent body started to build up the ache in the pit of her stomach, but she tried to stifle it. *Gosh, he must be thinking I am a complete wanton*, she thought to herself as she gave into the luxurious feeling of having her hair washed by a pair of strong male hands.

Ashok washed and rinsed her hair in silence, his face puckered in concentration. Annie turned around as she took the soap from Ashok's hands and in silence began to lather his body, starting on his back, down his arms, and finally she found her hands on his legs. He slowly turned around and took the soap from her. He set it aside as he pulled her close to him, and they made love once more in the shower. Later, he wrapped her up in a large bath towel before leading the way to the bedroom. A pot of coffee and two mugs waited on the bedside table.

'Ah, this is bliss.' Annie sighed as she took the first sip of the delicious hot beverage. 'You are good at this.'

'At what?' Ashok too took a sip as he sank down on the bed beside her. He had pulled on his shorts again, but his body was still damp from the shower.

'All this.' Annie made a sweeping gesture with her hand. 'Washing hair, making coffee. Pampering a woman the loveliest way possible.' She smiled.

'Well, I can just about stir a spoonful of instant in hot water. But believe it or not, this is the first time I have ever washed somebody else's hair. I am glad you feel pampered though. I want to take care of you. The best way possible.' He looked into her eyes, his face grave. He did not return her smile.

Annie suddenly felt breathless. She looked away from his eyes and, to avoid her confusion, took another sip of coffee.

'Thank you,' she managed at last. 'That is very gallant of you.'

'That was not my intention. I do not mean to be gallant. I mean it, every word.'

'Well, I . . .' Annie did not know what to say. She felt warm inside. In spite of their spending the night together with such abandon, this was something she felt was too much to handle. She desperately wanted to take a step back. But Ashok put down the cup and took her hands in both of his. She felt herself melting to the warm but firm touch of his hands.

'Annie, I don't know what to call this, but whatever it is that I feel for you—and I do feel for you—makes me want to take you in both my hands and put you away as one would to a piece of fragile china. I feel you might shatter into a thousand pieces if you are not handled delicately enough. It makes me want to protect you from everything—rain and hail and snow and muggers and loneliness . . .' He let go of her hands and thrust his hand through his hair in an agitated manner. 'I am making a mess of things, am I not?' he asked gloomily.

'That is the most romantic thing anyone has ever said to me,' she said in a trembling voice, keeping her eyes from filling up. Ashok looked startled.

'Was I being romantic?' he demanded. 'I was not aware of that. I was certainly not trying to be. I swear to you, that is the truth. That is exactly how I feel about you.'

Annie looked down to hide her confusion. Was he being sincere? One part of her wanted to believe in what he said and jump to the roof, yet another part of her was afraid to believe. She was also wary of this sudden intimacy between them; she was not sure where it was all leading.

'I am very flattered, Ashok, but I don't think I need looking after like the way you would look after a piece of fragile china. I am tough. I have seen life—made my share of mistakes, sure, but I have learned from them and am in a stage of my life where I am not ready to put all my trust into someone.'

'I hope you can trust me in this, Annie. I have never felt like this before. I have had another woman in the past, but I have never felt like this, and I have never been this physically or emotionally involved either—I don't know what to call it . . .' He came to a confused halt, shrugging.

'Connection?' Annie suggested under her breath.

'That's it. Connection. I feel I know you—all of you. And you know all of me.'

'I don't think it is possible for anybody to know another person totally, Ashok. There is always something that stays back.'

'And that is what I find so irresistible about you, Annie.' Ashok took her hands in his and bent down to look into her eyes, his expression earnest. 'You are like an enigma, a beautiful one, but a puzzle nonetheless. I find myself fascinated. I want to know more about you, what makes you tick. What you like and do not like. I want to know how you were as a child—whether you liked the rain or the snow, how you slept when you were little.'

Annie suddenly giggled. 'Well, that was not very elegant, I am afraid. I preferred to lift my right leg upon my little sister when I slept. She would be so mad.' She sobered. 'I do feel for you, Ashok. I honestly do. But we have so little time. I wish I had more time to get to know you better.'

'Stay.'

'What?'

'Stay. Don't leave today. You don't have to go to work or anything, so I think you can make time for us.'

Annie couldn't believe her ears. 'I do have work, whether or not I commute to an office, thank you. In case you have forgotten, I happen to be a very successful consultant. And my work is important to me.'

Ashok looked puzzled. 'Okay. I didn't mean to imply otherwise. But surely you can work from here? I want you to stay a few more days. We need the time together.'

But Annie was shaking her head even as he spoke. 'I can't, Ashok. I simply can't. Besides, there are other things. Rent to pay and taxes to file . . . numerous other things. I have a life out there—a life I have painstakingly built for myself. I just can't abandon all that.'

'All I am asking for is some time, maybe a few weeks.'

'And I want that as well. I don't want to go. You must see that. You do see that, don't you?' Annie lifted tortured eyes full of tears towards him. Ashok gathered her to him at once.

'Don't, please. I can't bear to see you cry, Annie.' He sighed.

Annie wept. 'I don't want to go. I want to stay here with you. But I can't. Oh god, I can't!'

'Hush, now. Shhhh. It is all right. It will be okay. You'll see.' Ashok soothed her, his hand smoothing her hair. Gently he tucked a runaway strand behind her ears, then he bent his mouth to hers. In a flash, they were kissing each other fiercely, clinging close as if even the mere thought of separating was unbearable. Ashok's hands smoothed the robe from her shoulders; eagerly she shrugged them off before reaching for him again.

If this was all the time she was going to have with him, then it was not the time to be coy, she decided as she surrendered to him one last time.

CHAPTER 13

Annie's stomach rumbled loudly in the silent room. She laughed. Ashok smiled. They lay sprawled on the bed, sated after the latest bout of lovemaking. Ashok looked at his wristwatch. It was almost noon. With a sigh, he heaved himself out of bed, gently untangling his hand from her hair, which was spread on the white pillow like amber silk.

'I love the colour of your hair,' he murmured. 'It reminds me of the wet sand on the beach.'

'It is mousy.' Annie grimaced.

'It is like silk.' Then he slapped her gently on her shoulders. 'Now, get ready, will you?'

'Why? Are you taking me somewhere?'

'I am going to fix lunch. Meet me at the kitchen.' He sauntered out of the bedroom.

Annie stretched her arms above her. Her body ached, but it was a pleasurable ache. The last time had been somewhat athletic, she remembered with a smile. She had been on top, slowly riding him, her hair loose and flowing all over him, driving him crazy. Or so she hoped. She was not used to taking the initiative, but the very thought of leaving him made her shed her inhibitions this one time.

She got out of bed and pulled on her clothes for the second time that day. Rummaging through her purse, she came up with a comb and a tube of lipstick. She untangled her hair and tied it back with a scrunchy, but after considering the rather startling shade of red lipstick, she decided against it. She didn't even remember buying such a shade, she thought, putting it back in her purse. Maybe it was a gift. She peered into the bathroom mirror, mentally grimacing at the pale light that did not help at all. It made her skin look pasty. Oh, well! She would have to do, Annie thought to herself, even if she yearned for a dash of make-up and a decent dollop of lip gloss. Squaring her shoulders, she went out of the room to look for Ashok.

There was nobody in the living room. The windows were streaming with sunlight, and the room already felt warm from the midday sun. She went over and drew the curtains against the harsh light. The room instantly felt cool. She shook her head at herself. *It won't do, girl. It won't do at all. Get out of here fast before you dig yourself deeper,* she thought, but then movements in the kitchen caught her attention. She moved curiously towards the source of the sounds coming from there.

Ashok was busy at the countertop. There were diced vegetables, and a pressure cooker was building up steam on the oven. He looked up and smiled at her when she entered. Annie didn't know what to make of him in an apron that had tiny cherries and apples printed all over it. He was wearing a faded T-shirt and a pair of denims, his feet thrust into comfortable mules. He looked devastatingly handsome in this new domestic avatar; Annie felt hopelessly inadequate compared to his looks. She also felt hopelessly drawn to him.

'Come on in and make yourself comfortable,' Ashok said, indicating the small table with two chairs tucked in. Annie drew up one and sat back, her arms on the table, to watch him cook.

'I thought you said you couldn't cook,' she remarked.

'I can't. Not really. But I can cook this one vegetable curry that I learned from my mother, and I can steam rice,' Ashok replied. 'Would you like to have something? Wine? I think I have some white left.'

Annie shook her head. 'I don't want wine in the middle of the day, thank you. But I would appreciate a glass of water.'

Ashok left the vegetables and went to the fridge at the corner of the kitchen. He took out a bottle of chilled water and put it on the table. He took out a glass tumbler from the overhead cabinets and put that on the table as well.

'You are quite domesticated,' Annie remarked, pouring out some water into the tumbler. She took a long sip; the cold water soothed her perched throat. 'For a man.'

'Ah, but that is stereotyping, I am afraid.' Ashok deftly gathered up the cut vegetables in a strainer and put them under the tap. He turned to her, his eyes sparkling. 'Why shouldn't a man be domesticated? We don't go about saying that a lady is quite "undomesticated" for a woman, now, do we?'

Annie laughed and shook her head. 'No, but I thought in India men were a pampered lot, first by their mothers and then by their girlfriends or wives.'

'Hmmm. So do you?'

'Do I what?'

'Intend to pamper me?'

'But I am not your . . . mother,' Annie finished, her eyes lighting up in mischief.

Ashok laughed. Annie drank in the sound of his deep-throated laughter. She was glad she could make him laugh. Maybe he would remember her as the foreign woman who was funny. She wanted him to remember her, no matter how. There was a hollow feeling in the pit of her stomach as she bantered with him lightly while he cooked lunch.

Afterwards, Ashok carried the food back to the dining area, where he set the table for two. He took out some cooked chicken—his aunt had sent it over, he explained to Annie—which she heated in the microwave. Annie found wine glasses in the kitchen; she decided to have some wine, seeing they were now having lunch and this type of food needed some wine to enhance its flavour. Ashok brought out the white wine, which they had with the rice, vegetables, and chicken curry.

'The vegetables are perfect,' Annie remarked as they ate. 'Soft and juicy, without being too spicy. I love these.'

'I am glad. It is a very basic recipe of mixed veggies. My mother was worried that I would go without having a decent meal by myself, so she insisted that I learn to cook this at least. She also pestered her sister enough that she makes sure to send me something or the other every other day. You will find my fridge stocked most of the time.'

'You also spend time with your relatives, don't you?' Annie put a forkful of the spicy chicken into her mouth, bracing herself for the onslaught of chillies. But it was surprisingly smooth. Ashok looked at her knowingly, his eyes twinkling.

'I do,' he said in answer to her question. 'My aunt lives here with her son and daughter-in-law. Her husband died when she was young, and she had to bring up my cousin all by herself. It was tough for her, but now she lives in retirement, enjoying cooking for her grandkid. I get to share her cooking, luckily for me.'

'And thanks to your mother,' Annie said solemnly.

'And thanks to my mother,' Ashok agreed.

And thus it went on. They talked about their families and friends, sharing memories and anecdotes. Annie told him about her childhood home, her sister who now lived in New York, and her parents, who had passed on. Ashok told her about his family, his parents in Punjab, and his brother in Mumbai. His cousin was a corporate executive with a multinational company, and his sister-in-law was a schoolteacher. They had one child, a girl. They exchanged notes on their relatives and their antics, her senile great-uncle who would pee in the flowerpot and his grandmother who would insist that there were two midget ghosts under her bed.

Both avoided any talk about their joint future. Later Ashok brought out ice cream from the fridge, which they had while sitting on the balcony after they had cleared away the dishes. Annie had wanted to help in washing them, but Ashok told her there was a maid who would take care of them. They sat on the rattan chairs on the balcony and relished the vanilla flavour, the cold stinging their mouths but feeling good against the warm sun.

Annie watched people pass by in the street below. It was teeming with traffic, motorbikes and cars jostling for space while buses honked impatiently.

'Difficult to imagine it was so quiet last night,' she commented.

'Well, this is the busiest time of the day.'

'My fellow travellers are having a picnic today.'

'Are they?'

'Uh-huh. Nancy wanted me to join, but I told her to go ahead without me.'

'Would you rather go there?'

Was there a trace of terseness in his tone? Annie wondered. 'I would most certainly not,' she answered easily. 'I much prefer to be here.' She smiled.

Ashok relaxed. 'I am glad of that,' he said simply, taking her hand. It felt as if it were the most natural thing on earth, him taking her hand casually, his touch light but intimate. Annie leaned deeper into the cushions with a sigh of contentment. They sat there like that, holding hands, watching the street below. The silence between them felt strangely comfortable. *Would it be like this with him?* Annie wondered. This sense of peace and contentment was something her soul had craved for so passionately. Who knew that she would find it with this man—in this wonderful foreign country so far away from her own? She could cry from the unfairness of it all. She wanted to be in familiar surroundings; she wanted to be home. But she wanted Ashok to be with her. And India fascinated her. She had found such joy, vibrancy, and life in this country of contradictions, where tradition and modernity existed side by side; there was complete absence of any conflict whatsoever. She wanted to explore more of this wonderful ancient land, but she had to go back home. She had a flight to catch.

Slowly she took her hand from his and stood up. 'I have to go,' she said softly, her voice laden with regret.

Ashok looked at her in silence, his eyes searching her face for something, she knew not what. Then he nodded.

'Let me get my keys.'

CHAPTER 14

IT WAS ALMOST THREE IN the afternoon when Annie reached her hotel. The drive had been almost entirely in silence; Ashok was concentrating on the heavy midday traffic, and Annie was too miserable to make conversation. She wanted to bawl her eyes out but was loath to make a scene. So she stoically looked out the window, the cars and people passing unseen before her eyes. As the car came to a halt, she came out of her reverie with a start.

'We are here,' Ashok said in a low voice. He seemed subdued.

'Already?' Annie wanted to shout, but she just bit her lip and nodded grimly. What was the point? She knew this was bound to end; there was no way she could stay here and allow this to continue forever. She had to face reality.

'Yes,' she said now and made to get out of the car. Ashok put his hand over hers. She looked for a moment where her hand—rather paler than his—lay on the car seat with his much larger one covering it, then looked up at him. Ashok was looking at her.

'I will see you again,' he vowed softly.

Her lips trembled as tears threatened to spill over. 'How? Tell me, how?' She shook her head and turned away, her vision blurred by tears. 'It is too much,' she whispered.

'I will.' Ashok's voice was soft but determined. 'Just remember that.' He squeezed her hand before releasing it at last.

'Will you come to the airport? You know, to see me off?' Annie refused to put too much hope in his words; the distance was too great, and she didn't mean only just the kilometres.

Ashok shook his head slightly. 'I hate goodbyes, but if you want me to, I will take you. Remember, I shall see you again, so there is no point in dragging this moment out. Go home and settle. I shall come for you. Just believe that.'

Annie did not say another word. She got out of the car and walked through the main porch. She did not look back because she did not trust herself to not make a fool of herself.

The interior of the hotel was cool with the shades drawn at that time of the day. Annie could not spot anyone from her group. Maybe they were not back from their picnic yet. She was glad for that small mercy. Making polite small talk was out of the question now. She went straight up to her room and hauled her case out to start packing. There was quite some packing to do anyway. Methodically she folded and tucked and wrapped, her mind a void, not allowing herself to think further than the task at hand. Her shoes went there, and her scarves here. The jewellery in the small box and the gifts for home went in the inside pocket. Finally, she fell on to the bed in a state of exhaustion, falling asleep almost immediately, unconsciously relieved for the reprieve it provided. Unknown to her, tears streamed down her cheeks even as she slept.

When she awoke, it was dark, and somebody was moving in the room. Disoriented from her deep slumber, she called out, 'Ashok?'

The lights came on, making her squint against their suddenly harsh glare. 'It's me.' It was Nancy. They had come back from the picnic. 'You are back.'

'Yes. Yes, I am back.' Annie sat up in bed, pushing back her hair from her face. 'I have finished packing.'

'I have too. At least most of it. Only some small items need to be put in.' Nancy sat on the chair, kicking off her shoes. 'I have some time though. I start a couple of hours later than you.'

'Uh-huh.' Annie went to the bathroom. Her eyes felt as if they had sand under the lids. She splashed cold water on her face, gasping as the cold stung. Her face looked swollen and red.

'Annie! Whatever is the matter? You look terrible!' Nancy took the first good look at her face and was immediately concerned.

'I think I got a touch of the sun,' Annie said. The truth was she felt terrible. She wanted to pound her fists to the ground, kick up the dust, and howl in agony. But she smiled and made polite talk with Nancy as she chatted on about her day at the picnic. It was not Nancy's fault, whatever had happened. It was nobody's fault but her own stupid luck—fate, karma, whatever—that she found the man of her dreams, and the situation was just beyond hope. No, Nancy was not to be blamed at all.

Annie had an early dinner at the restaurant all by herself. Some of their tour members had decided to travel to other parts of the country, while some others were leaving the day after. Nancy was leaving the same night, but as she said, her flight was a couple of hours later. She would be joining the others for a late dinner and dancing at a popular nightclub nearby.

As she chewed on the food that tasted like sawdust, Annie thought about the last few days. This was the first time she had travelled alone this far. When she had planned the trip, she had no idea how she was to manage by herself. She was going back more confident and buoyant. India was wonderful; everybody had been wonderful. She only wished she had Ashok with her, but of course, that was not to be. Maybe she would visit the continent next time, she thought. Who knows, she might even get to know some interesting people there as well, she pondered whimsically.

After finishing dinner, she went up to her room. There was some time before her taxi arrived. Nancy was taking a shower, so Annie spent the time calling Becky back home.

'Annie? Honey, where are you? Are you home already?' Becky was her affable best, as always.

'No. I am still in India. But my flight will leave in a few hours. I thought I would call you before I leave.'

'You thought right. Tell me, how are things there? After you left, I looked up New Delhi on the Net and—my gosh, Annie! It is a terrible place! Women are not safe there at all. I am so glad you are unhurt and coming back intact, you know.'

Annie had to laugh. She couldn't help it. Becky sounded so hopelessly out of her depth that it was funny. 'Becky! That is not true at all. This is a marvellous place. The people have been wonderful. I did not feel unsafe for one moment. They took very good care of me.'

They chatted for a few minutes after that. One of Becky's dogs was about to have a litter, and she was excited about that. Annie rang off as it was almost time for her to leave.

The taxi took her through the busy streets of Delhi towards the airport. This was another part of the city, quite unlike the ancient, charming portion she had explored with Ashok. The memories brought a lump to her throat. Would she ever see him again? Resolutely, she shoved thoughts of him from her mind and concentrated on the journey ahead of her. Even then, she could not help but cast a look around her when she got out of the taxi. All the while, loading a cart with her luggage, she hoped to see his face. But no matter how hard she looked, there was not a tall man with sparkling eyes and dark hair in the crowd. So much for his promise to see her again, she thought with a stab in her heart as she went through the doors of the international terminal. Just then, her phone went off with a text from Ashok: 'Have a safe flight, my love. I will see you soon. Love you always xoxoxox.'

The flight was uneventful, except that Annie could barely control her tears through the length of it. Sometimes they spilled over, but mostly she kept her eyes closed and tried to avoid any conversation whatsoever. When the meals arrived, she accepted them, loath to create a fuss, but she barely touched them. Mostly, she dozed. It was easier to cope with the pain that way.

Why did Ashok say that he would see her if he had no intention of keeping his word?

She was to arrive in New York, and from there, she would catch a connecting flight to Florida. It was cloudy when her flight arrived, matching her mood. There was some time till her next flight, so she decided to get herself pampered before she arrived home. She took a cab to the nearest salon.

The beauty expert at the salon, a thin man in his fifties, raised his brows when he saw her.

'Darling! Where have you been? You look like a toughened nut. All that brown! I envy you.' He seated her at a chair, covering her with a white plastic sheet as he scrutinized her fussily.

'I am just back from a vacation. India.'

'Oh! How wonderful! That explains your lovely tan.' He picked up a tuft of her long hair between his fingers. 'But these are too dry and sunburnt. It has to go. Luckily, you have the bone structure to carry a shorter style.'

But Annie was shaking her head even as he spoke. 'I can't have it shortened, thank you. Just a spa and a shampoo, please.' Ashok loved her long hair; she could not bear to part with it. Not yet anyway. It was too soon.

The beautician shrugged. 'Whatever you prefer, dear.' He then set about to expertly layer and massage and slather, after which he gave her hair a thorough wash. About two hours later, her hair felt soft and silky after the blow-dry. She smiled.

'Thank you. That was marvellous. I needed that.' It was true. She felt relaxed after the session at the salon. She peered into the mirror for a closer look. Big eyes looked back at her from the mirror. Loose strands of lustrous hair lay lazily over her shoulders and neck, giving her a faintly morose look. She shrugged. She would do.

Considering everything, she was doing fine for now. She thanked the stylist, paid and tipped him, and left the salon. Time to face the real world. She was home.

CHAPTER 15

THE SCENES OUTSIDE FELT SURREAL to Annie as her taxi sped past the familiar landmarks of her hometown. It was morning, and the sun was already shining brightly, the palm trees along the marine drive swaying gently in the sea breeze. How many times had she driven past the same road, seen the same trees, and felt the same sea breeze on her face ever since she had moved here so many years ago? Yet as she looked out now, it all seemed so new, foreign almost. She was not sure she would be able to sink into the life she knew before she had gone to India. The fascinating country had changed her; she sensed it instinctively, but she was not sure how. *Oh well, I will find out soon enough, I guess*, she thought as the taxi took the turn to her home.

The sight of the white low-ceilinged bungalow that was her home was a relief. The small white house was fenced with white picket, which guarded a small but well-kept green lawn. Its lush fullness was broken only by the sole oleander tree that stood at one corner. It was in full bloom now, the pink flowers adding a dash of colour in the starkness of the green-and-white landscape. As Annie walked down the path to her door, she could smell the watered grass; her neighbour had kindly agreed to water it while she was gone. She mentally made a note to thank him later. Fishing inside her purse, she came up with the keys and finally entered her home. Just then, her cell phone rang. It was Ashok, calling to see if she had gotten home safely. They spoke for a few minutes, and then Ashok said he had to go, but not before he said to Annie in that deep voice that she loved so much, 'Annie, I love you, and I miss you a lot already.'

Annie was silent for a second before she responded, 'I love and miss you too, Ashok.'

Inside, it was not quite so picturesque. There was a fine layer of dust on every surface, and the hall seemed gloomy, with the blinds drawn against the sun. Annie grimaced and went to the window, throwing it open and letting the sun and the breeze in. She put down her luggage on the living room carpet and went straight to the broom closet. A few minutes later, sounds of the vacuum cleaner filled the air.

After she had finished vacuuming and dusting every spot until they shone, she decided to go out for a sandwich. All the work had made her hungry, but the larder was empty. She decided to visit the stores before coming back. She had a burger at the local deli and visited the store for some basic groceries.

'Annie. Hi! You looked super tanned. How was your trip?'

'Hi, Trixie.' Annie smiled. Trixie was her neighbour; she lived a few houses down the street. 'The trip was great.'

'When did you get back?'

'An hour or so ago.' Annie grinned. 'It feels good to be home.' And she meant it, she realized with faint surprise.

It did feel good. She had expected to be heartbroken and miserable, but the familiar sights and sounds of her home were welcome too. She had not realized how much she had missed it.

'I bet India was amazing,' Trixie was saying.

'It was.'

'Well, we'll catch up later. I have to go now. Bye.' Trixie pushed her cart towards the checkout counter.

'Bye, Trixie.' Annie went back to her shopping. She put milk, fruits, and cereals in her cart; she would need them for breakfast first thing the next morning.

She was fast asleep as soon as she hit the pillow, the jet lag finally catching up with her.

When she woke up, it was almost midday. After a long shower, she scrunched up her hair and threw on a pair of faded denims and an old T-shirt. After going to the kitchen, she fixed herself an omelette and had a glass of milk with it. Then she opened her laptop to check her mail. Most of her assignments came via the Internet, and she wanted to start working right away. She did not want to give herself time to miss Ashok; she would come apart if she allowed herself to think of him. The pain was still too raw. She only hoped that it would become bearable with time.

There were quite a few interesting projects waiting for her in her mail. She eagerly delved into them and, after an hour or so, was busily tapping away numbers on her laptop. She stopped only when her stomach rumbled in protest. The sun was going down, and the sky outside was a pinkish hue. She gazed at the beautiful magic light for a few moments, and then suddenly her eyes filled with tears quickly running down her cheeks. The sky reminded her of the day she was at Agra, visiting the Taj Mahal. Ashok had surprised her there. It seemed so far away now, so long ago. Was it only a few days back? It seemed another lifetime. Would she ever go back there? Not in this lifetime. People like her did not take transcontinental vacations every month—even every year. Angrily she brushed away the tears and got up from the chair. The sooner she forgot about him, the better. There were chores to be done, things to do. She had to unpack, and there was the laundry to tackle. She was glad for the workload; it would help her stay busy and stop thinking about him.

So her pattern fell into a familiar pace the following days. She was up early, doing her laundry, cooking, cleaning, and washing. She worked on her projects at a furious pace until dinner time, then fixed herself dinner and promptly fell asleep afterwards. She allowed herself no time to think about what had happened. She did not think at all, except about work, and she worked her body to exhaustion.

This was the only way she could cope.

A week later, her cell phone rang. Annie was out in the garden, watering the lawn. Hearing her phone ring inside, she left the watering pipe and ran indoors, her heart beating furiously. Was it . . . ? No, it was Becky. She tried to stifle her disappointment as she took the call. She also felt a bit guilty; she had not rung Becky up since she had returned.

'Becky. Hi.'

'Annie! I am not sure if I should be angry with you.' Becky sounded anything but angry though.

'I know. I should have called, but . . .'

'Are you okay, honey? You sound kind of subdued. Is everything all right?'

'Everything is all right, Becky. In fact, I . . .' Annie's voice failed her as she choked back tears. Heavens, this would never do. What was the matter with her? She was okay a moment ago.

Even as she struggled to regain her composure amid Becky's concerned queries, Annie knew what was wrong. She missed Ashok terribly. Hearing Becky's friendly voice after so many days finally broke the dam inside her. Tears spilled down her cheeks, unchecked. She put her fist to her mouth to stem the howl that threatened to tear from within her; her insides felt as if they were ripping apart, so bad was the pain.

'Annie? Honey, what's wrong? Are you okay? Talk to me, baby, please.' Becky's concerned voice reached her ears, but all she could do was manage a few choked sobs. 'That's it. I am coming over.' Becky hung up.

'No, no, Becky . . .' Annie started, but the connection was gone. Slowly she put down the phone and went to sit on the rocking chair on the porch. Maybe this was for the better; God knew she needed somebody. She had needed somebody since the day she came home, and Becky was the nearest thing to family she had there.

It would feel good to see Becky again.

Becky arrived the very next day. She had driven with her three dogs, and they jumped right out on to the lawn and started to sniff around. Annie hurried out to greet them, and they jumped on her too.

'They are a bit excited,' Becky explained. 'They love to go on long drives, and the new place has made them hyper.'

They spent a few minutes calming the dogs. They finally flopped on the cool shade of the porch, their tongues lolling out in the midday heat. Annie brought out lemonades, which they shared with the pooches.

'It feels so good to see you, Becky. I missed you.' Annie took a long sip out of her glass. The cool drink went down her parched throat, making her want to purr in contentment. She felt much better today, almost in control.

'Right. Now tell me. What was yesterday all about?' Becky put down her empty glass on the low table and leaned back. Annie stole a look at her face and, seeing the determination there, decided to cut to the chase. It was not easy to fool Becky anyway; she had a way of extracting the truth when she had her mind to it. For all her easy manner, she could be quite the dragon when she wanted to be.

'You remember Ashok? I told you about him,' Annie began.

'Of course I remember him. The hotel manager you contacted when you thought of going to India. But then you changed your mind and went through a tour operator instead.'

'Yes, well, I met him when I went to Delhi. I told you about that, didn't I?'

'Yes, you did. Why?'

'I believe I have made a fool of myself, Becky.'

Becky's eyes went round. 'He didn't dupe you out of your money, did he? India is a place where things like that can happen. I read about it somewhere.'

'No, no, nothing like that. And I don't know what you read and where, but I found the people there quite friendly. We never had any problems like that there.'

'Then what—oh my god! He didn't try anything with you? I mean, you know—stuff? God, Annie, did he assault you?'

'No!' Annie almost laughed in spite of her misery. 'God, Becky, I should think at my age I would know what to do if something like that happened to me.'

'Huh! You are the most unlikely person to go to the police, if you ask me. Now, if it were me—'

'I know, you would teach him a lesson he wouldn't forget in a hurry. But it is nothing like that. He did not do anything. I made a fool of myself. Oh, Becky, I think I have fallen in love with him!' The last part came out in a wail.

'Honey!' Becky's arms went around her. 'Now, calm down. How did all this happen? Tell me. Here, take this.'

Annie took the proffered tissue and dabbed her eyes before blowing her nose. Becky waited patiently till she found her composure. The dogs waited too.

'You are in love, baby? But that is wonderful. That is good news. After that nasty Zack, it will do you good to find a man again.'

'But that's it, Becky. He is not my man. I don't think he even knows. And I am sure he doesn't love me.' Annie felt like crying again and bit her trembling lips for control.

'All right. We will talk later. Right now, I am going to fix you lunch. The boys need their meal too. It is past their lunchtime. Come on, babies, inside with Mama.' Becky whistled to the dogs, and they jumped up to obediently trot after her into the house. Annie shook her head. Becky was a force of nature; it was futile to try to stop her. She got up from her chair, gathered up the empty glasses and jug, and followed Becky inside.

CHAPTER 16

AN HOUR LATER, THE DOGS snoozed under their feet as they nursed their second helpings of lemonade of the day. They had just finished their lunch of salad and delicious cucumber and butter sandwiches that Becky had fixed. They were now sprawled on the couch in the living room. Annie told Becky all—how she had met Ashok for the first time at the hotel, how they had made love, and later, how she felt when she had to leave him. She left out nothing, her voice cracking at times and softening at others when she remembered how good it felt to be with him, how right it all seemed. Becky listened with attention, her eyes on Annie's animated face as she talked.

'He said he would see me again, but I am sure that was just his way of softening the blow,' Annie was saying now.

'What blow?' Becky asked.

'Well, you know. The blow of rejection. I think it was a relief to him that I was leaving. Maybe I was just an exotic experience to him, an affair with a foreigner. She would go back eventually, and so it all worked out well for him. Whereas I, fool that I am . . .' She choked.

'Maybe it was an exotic affair for you too. How do you know it wasn't? A holiday in an exotic foreign country, a handsome man, and no strings attached. These things happen.'

'I love him. The very thought of him brings me such joy and such pain together . . . I have never felt anything like this in my life.'

'Then you must believe him. Loving means to trust, doesn't it? He has said he will find a way to see you. You have to believe that.'

'If it were that simple. Why hasn't he even called then? It's been almost a week now.'

'Why don't you call him? The phone works both ways, you know. Call him, talk to him, and find out what he plans.'

Annie shook her head. 'I can't. I am too scared.'

'Oh, Annie.' Becky sounded impatient. 'You can be too timid for your own good, you know. That was why you tolerated Zack for so long.' She shook her head. 'You will never be happy unless you find out. You know that as well. You should call him.'

And as far as Becky was concerned, that was that.

They went out in the afternoon. Becky insisted that they take the dogs to the waterfront. They ran and frolicked in the sand as the sun went down until they were too exhausted to move. Later they had ice cream, which the dogs enjoyed to the hilt.

'I am afraid you spoil them,' Annie commented.

'I do, don't I?' Becky grinned unrepentantly. 'They bring so much joy to me. This is but little that I give them back.'

'You need somebody in your life. I mean, they are great dogs, but you need someone who will be your soulmate.'

'We live in hope, my beauty. We live in hope.'

Becky drove back after dinner. They had had their meal at the local deli, and she dropped Annie off near her home before saying bye. As Annie slowly walked the street that led to her house, her head bent, she mentally traced her steps back to the weeks she had left behind in India. She could see Ashok as if he were there right before her eyes, his black hair slightly ruffled in the breeze, his teasing smile, the way he cocked his head in attention when he seemed fascinated by something.

A car whizzed past. Some tropical flower spread its scent in the air, mingling with the smell of the sea. Annie sighed. She wished she did not have to go back to the empty house. It would feel terribly empty after the day with Becky and her dogs. She remembered Becky's advice. She wanted Annie to call Ashok, but she wasn't sure she could do it. What if he didn't want to talk to her? Then she remembered how he had pleaded with her to stay; maybe he wanted her after all. Annie wished she knew what went on in his mind. This was agony.

Why hadn't he called?

She had reached her home. Annie fished inside her beach bag and hunted around for her keys, cursing under her breath as she looked for them. Finally, she found them; they had sunk to the bottom. As she was about to turn the key in the lock, she noticed somebody approaching her. It was too dark to properly see the features, but it was a man—a tall man, his hair ruffling in the breeze. Annie's heart leaped to her throat. It couldn't be! She was hallucinating. He was a few thousand miles away, across the Pacific. It wasn't him.

'Hello, Annie,' Ashok said in an even voice.

Annie stared at him dully. She couldn't bring out a reply to his greeting even if she wanted to. She couldn't believe her eyes.

Ashok took a few steps towards her until he was close. He took her hands in his. 'Aren't you going to say something?'

'Say what?' Annie managed to croak.

'Something like how glad you are that I am here would do, for starters.'

Annie pulled her hands away from his and turned towards the door. She couldn't trust herself to do the right thing; she wanted to yell and cry and laugh at the same time. Her insides were churning up all kinds of emotions. Wordlessly she motioned him inside. Ashok laughed softly and followed her into her home.

Annie put the keys on the table beside the door and looked back at Ashok. He stood in her doorway, looking at her, his body completely still. He was wearing a light-grey sweater and a pair of dark denims, his feet encased in soft loafers. His hair was brushed back from his high forehead, gleaming in the evening light. He brought a lump to her throat. She dropped the keys on the table beside the door and took a step towards him. Suddenly she was in his arms; she hugged him back as tightly. Their mouths fused together hotly, each straining to get closer to the other. It was as if the last few days were not there.

It feels just the same was Annie's last coherent thought before Ashok kicked the door shut and carried her over to the couch.

It was much later when Annie became aware of her surroundings. She had dozed off, and when she opened her eyes, the living room was in complete darkness. For a moment or two, she lay there on the couch, puzzled. She could hear the crickets outside. There was no moon, so she could not see very well into the room, but she could feel a warm and hard body against her. She frowned—and then it came back to her in a rush. Ashok. He had come to her door, and they had made torrid love on the couch. Her face burned when she recalled how she had gone for him; he must think she was a complete wanton. She tried to sit up fast but found that she could hardly move. He was half-sprawled over her. Carefully she started to push him aside so that she could get up. Feeling her way in the darkness, she pulled on her sundress and switched on the lamp. Ashok lay on his stomach, one arm hanging down the couch. *Well, that much has not changed!* she thought tartly. He always slept on his stomach.

Ashok lifted his head lazily from where he had fallen into a deep slumber on the couch. He frowned, looking puzzled at first, and then smiled when he spotted Annie sitting on an armchair opposite him. Lifting his arm, he beckoned her to him.

'Come here.'

But Annie shook her head. She was not about to give in to his charms so easily this time. She cringed when she thought about her behaviour earlier; what had possessed her to jump on him like that? But even as she asked herself, she knew the answer to that. She was hopelessly in love with him. Nothing compared to what she felt this time.

When she shook her head adamantly, Ashok sighed and lifted himself up to sit on the couch. He picked up his trousers where they had fallen on the floor and pulled them on, leaving his chest bare. His hair was rumpled; he looked good enough to eat to Annie. She averted her eyes. It would not do to fall for that charm again.

'Annie,' Ashok said softly.

'What are you doing here, Ashok?' Annie blurted out at last.

'I told you I would see you again, didn't I?'

'Yes, but—what do you want?'

'What do you mean? Aren't you happy to see me?' There was a trace of hurt in his voice. Annie chose to ignore it.

'Of course I am glad to see you. God, didn't I prove that amply the moment I saw you?'

'Do you regret making love, Annie?' Ashok asked in a low voice.

Annie shook her head. 'It's not that. I . . . I have missed you terribly these last few days, Ashok.'

Ashok smiled and leaned forward to take her hand.

'But I need to know,' Annie continued. 'Where do we go from here? How do you feel about me? Do you have any plans for the future? There are so many unresolved questions between us. I feel I don't know whether I am standing on my feet or head.'

Ashok let go of her hand and leaned back. He pushed his hair back from his forehead and then allowed his hand to flop back on his lap. Annie wished she could stop her hungry gaze from following his rippling muscles. As it was, she almost missed his low voice when he spoke.

'I love you.'

She tore her eyes from his shoulders. 'I—*what*?'

'I said I love you.'

CHAPTER 17

Annie went numb. She sat there for a full minute, staring ahead. Ashok looked at her in amusement, which turned into concern after some time.

'Annie? Say something.'

Annie turned to look at him. To her mortification, she felt tears streaming freely down her cheeks.

'Hey! Hey!'

In an instant, she was gathered up and held close. 'I never dreamt that loving you would cause such distress,' Ashok mused, not without a trace of humour.

Annie laughed shakily. 'Not distress, silly. These are tears of happiness. I love you too, you see. Oh god, I love you so much.'

Ashok used his thumbs to gently wipe the traces of tears from the corners of her eyes, and then he bent to kiss her. After some time, Annie pulled away.

'I feel like such a fool,' she confessed. 'I could never cry gracefully. In the movies, the heroines look so pretty when they cry. I get all blotched and red-nosed.' She gave a little self-conscious laugh, rubbing her eyes like a small child.

'You look beautiful,' Ashok said. 'You are the most beautiful thing I have ever set my eyes upon. From the very first time I saw you, I was struck by your beauty.'

'When did you know that you love me?' Annie wanted to know.

'I am not sure. It kind of crept upon me, you see. I was terribly attracted to you from the moment I set my eyes upon you. I could hardly be away from you.'

'Was that why you followed us to the Taj Mahal?'

'That and I wanted to experience Taj with you. I suppose that should have clued me in. As it was, the very idea of you going away caused me crippling pain. Then I knew. This is it.' He looked down at her, still locked in his arms, and darted a quick kiss on her brow. 'Now, tell me when you knew.'

'I knew when, even after coming home, I could not concentrate on anything. Your face, your voice—they kept coming to me. There were times I had to stop whatever I was doing just to get over the pain.'

They talked and loved and were completely oblivious to the time till Ashok's stomach emitted a loud growl.

'I am so sorry!' Annie exclaimed. 'I should have thought about it earlier.'

Quickly she went to the kitchen and got busy. Ashok followed her there, observing her fix omelettes and a sandwich for him with quick hands.

'It feels so right, seeing you fixing dinner for me,' he remarked mildly.

It felt right to Annie too, but she said nothing except 'You must find it hopelessly inadequate after all the beautiful food you are accustomed to at home. I know I miss it, and I was there only for a short while.'

Two strong arms came around her middle. 'I love whatever you rustle up for me,' he said in a low voice, nuzzling her hair.

Much later, when Ashok was sprawled out on the bed, did it occur to Annie; what was he doing here in Florida? It occurred to her that she was so ecstatic to see him here that she had forgotten to ask him. She had not noticed any luggage with him. Had he put up somewhere else? She wanted answers, but he was exhausted—jet lag, maybe. She didn't have the heart to interrupt his sleep. After some time, she went to the bathroom to change and then slid into bed beside him under the covers.

When she opened her eyes, the sun was up, and the first thing she remembered was last evening, how Ashok had showed up at her doorstep. They had made love twice, and then he had gone to sleep on her bed. She turned to look at him. The bed was empty. Jumping out of bed, she peered into the hall; there was nobody there. Her heart sank—until she saw the note on the pillow. Her hands trembled as she picked it up and opened its folds with unsteady fingers.

'Darling, I have to start my day early. I have some meetings to attend to. I shall be back in the evening. Love, Ashok.'

She put back the note on the table, her expression thoughtful. He would be back. He said so in the note. But what if—she jumped as her cell phone rang. As she rushed to pick up the phone, it occurred to her that she didn't know his current number.

It was Becky. Annie tried to keep the disappointment from her voice as she answered it.

'Hi, Becky.'

'Well, I have reached home, safe and sound. Thought I would give you a tinkle, seeing that you are so anxious about me and all.'

Annie grimaced. 'I am sorry. I should have checked. But I was so preoccupied since last evening that—I am sorry, baby.'

'What's the matter? Everything okay?' Becky asked sharply.

'I am not sure.' Annie sat down on the chair beside the door. 'You see, Ashok turned up yesterday at my doorstep.'

'Come again?'

'Ashok. He is here in Miami. And he came to see me yesterday.'

'No! Seriously? What is he doing here? Anyway, it is the best thing that could happen to you—seeing that you were pining for him and all.'

'I was not pining for him,' Annie protested.

'Honey, birds will sing about you one day. But what is he doing here? And how did he know where to find you?'

'That was easy. He had my address from the emails I exchanged with him. As for what he is doing, I have no idea. He says he loves me, Becky.'

'But that is great!'

'I am not sure. He left this morning. He left a note saying he will be back by evening.'

'So get yourself into your sexiest negligee and cook him a great dinner. Then have some action at last.'

'We had some action,' Annie confessed, blushing. 'I don't know what to do now.'

'Listen, honey, do you want to be with him?'

'Of course!'

'Then grab this with both hands. Don't hesitate, don't doubt.'

'I don't want to get hurt. Not again. And this time, I know I will not survive, Becky. I love him too much. This is like nothing before.'

'I understand. But think about it. Your rewards will also be like nothing before. Don't you think it's worth the risk?'

They talked a few minutes after that, and then Becky hung up. Annie spent the rest of the day in a state of anxiety and anticipation alternatively. It was almost dinner time when the buzzer rang. She almost flew to open the door.

CHAPTER 18

'MISS ME?' ASHOK ASKED AFTER he had finished thoroughly kissing her.

'Not one bit,' Annie laughed.

Ashok was here in Miami on restaurant business and was staying at a hotel down town with his aunt who had accompanied him to see her son who was in college here; he had rented a car for his use.

'Minx.' He handed her a small package neatly wrapped in white satin with a silver bow. 'It reminded me of you.'

'Oh! What is it?'

'Open it. I hope you like it.'

With trembling, impatient fingers, Annie tore open the package. Inside was a delicate silver chain with an amber pendant shaped like a star.

'It is beautiful,' Annie whispered. She looked up at him, her eyes shining. 'Thank you.'

'So you like it then?'

'I love it.'

Ashok took it from her fingers and put it around her neck. Pushing her hair to one shoulder, he fastened it. Then he put her hair back in place and turned her around.

'The colour of the pendant reminded me of your hair.' He smiled. 'Now, shall we go out for dinner? I am rather famished.'

'Oh. But I have to change. Can you give me a few minutes?'

Annie dashed to her bedroom. Pulling out the indigo printed dress she had bought at Rajasthan, she shook it out and hung it before applying make-up and doing her hair. She brushed the heavy tresses back from her forehead and used a hair clip to hold them in place. A hint of coral blusher brought out her cheekbones. Lastly, she put on the dress, carefully arranging the pendant so that it nestled at the base of her neck. It was rather warm, so she stuck to strappy sandals, and she was ready.

As she came out of her room, Ashok looked up from the newspaper he was browsing through. His eyes glinted appreciatively, but he said nothing.

'Where do you want to go?' Annie asked as they left her house.

'I am at a loss here. You tell me where we can find a decent meal. Not too expensive as I have to watch my wallet.'

Annie laughed. 'You don't have to worry about that. Here, you are my guest.' But Ashok was firmly shaking his head.

'I don't believe in making the lady pay, Annie. I will pay.'

'We can go Dutch. You know, split the check.'

'Not acceptable. Now, where do you think you can take me?'

Annie sighed inwardly but did not argue, though she resolved to share at least part of the check later on. 'There is a place nearby that serves great Mexican food. We can go there. It is a little like Indian food—they too use some spice—and I like the ambience.'

'Mexican it is then.'

They had a leisurely meal at the restaurant, accompanied by red wine. Ashok chose to have rice and chicken while Annie preferred fish. The place had small tables covered with red-and-white-check cloths, and a posy of pretty daisies adorned the centrepiece. The food was good, the wine delectable, and conversation flowed easily. They talked about everything; it never ceased to amaze Annie how much she could actually share with Ashok. They had no idea how much time had passed until his phone rang.

'I am sorry. I have to take this one,' Ashok said when he saw the caller number.

'Sure,' Annie said. 'I have to pay a visit to the loo anyway.'

She made her way towards the washroom at the back of the restaurant. She refreshed her lip gloss and ran a brush through her hair before making her way back to the table.

Ashok was still talking on the phone. She could not help but overhear part of the conversation.

'I have a few more minutes to go, and then I will be home. I promise.' Seeing Annie, he smiled but went on with his call. 'Yes, I do remember. Have I ever not? I shall certainly take you shopping tomorrow . . . Now go to bed and don't worry. I will be home by midnight.' He laughed and hung up.

'Sorry. That was my aunt. My father's elder sister.'

'You seem to have many aunts,' Annie observed.

Ashok shrugged. 'Well, you know us Indians. We have a large family. She stays near Delhi, and her son, my cousin brother, is a student at the University of Miami. She travelled with me to see him.'

'Why are you here, Ashok? I never got around to asking you.'

'I have to attend a conference on hotel management. My hotel has chosen me to represent them, which is a great thing for me. So it is a part-official and part-personal visit for me.'

'When you said you would see me again, did you know that you would be coming here?'

'Talks were on. I was not sure, but I had hoped.'

'I would like to meet your aunt. And your cousin. Maybe I can take her shopping tomorrow?' Annie smiled.

But Ashok did not smile back. In fact, he looked uncomfortable. After a small pause, he said, 'I am not sure about that. My aunt is a bit old-fashioned and . . .'

Annie frowned in confusion. 'What do you mean? You are allowed to have a friend, aren't you?'

'Of course. It's not that. But seeing you, she might sense something. She has the smelling power of a Labrador.' He tried to joke, but Annie wasn't smiling.

'She might sense what? That we are lovers? That you love me and I love you? You said you love me.'

'And I do. I love you.'

'But you are afraid that your aunt might come to know of that?' Annie was getting more and more agitated. 'You want to be my lover but keep your family in the dark? Is that it?'

The waiter came with the check. As Ashok took out his card, Annie snatched the check from him. 'I can pay my way, thank you very much.'

'Don't be childish, please. I will never allow you to pay.'

'This is the US of A, Ashok. Not India. Women do not expect to be protected or subjugated here. We pay for our meals.'

'Annie, you are overreacting.' Calmly Ashok plucked the check back from her trembling fingers and put his card and the check back into the folder. The waiter appeared at his shoulder and silently withdrew with it. Annie felt tears of rage prickle her eyes.

'So now what are you plans?' she asked, not without considerable sarcasm. 'A final fuck and then go back to your relative?'

'Please don't talk like that. It is demeaning.'

'For whom? I feel demeaned already. Forgive me for my language, will you?'

'Annie,' Ashok sighed and reached for her hands. She snatched them out of his reach and placed them on her lap.

'What did you tell her about yesterday anyway? It must have taken some creative explanation on your part.' She tried to steady her voice.

'Nothing. She didn't ask, and I told her nothing. Look, my people are modern and tolerant. They appreciate that I am a grown male. I stay on my own in Delhi, for God's sake. They understand that I might have a relationship . . .'

'But not with me, is that it? A foreigner, divorced twice, older than you . . .'

Ashok shook his head impatiently. 'It will not matter.' The waiter came back with the folder and the card. After leaving a tip, Ashok pulled back her chair, and they left.

'Ultimately, my choice is my own,' he continued. 'But if my aunt smells a rat tomorrow, it might create an unnecessary fuss, which I am hoping to avoid.'

'I see. I would like to walk back home, please. Alone.'

'Don't be silly. I will come with you. This is not ending here. You are still angry.'

They walked back to her house in silence. Ashok had tried to make conversation a few times, but Annie was too upset to make polite chit-chat. As she fished in her purse for her keys, a strange calm settled over her. She would show him. She could be as civil as he was when things went the wrong way. She would be polite and gracious even if her heart felt like shattering.

'Would you like some coffee?' she asked with frigid civility as she crossed the threshold.

'What I would like is to beat some sense into you.' Ashok followed her, his face grim.

'That's right. Beat me, why don't you? Everybody else has.'

He sighed. 'That's not what I meant, and you know that. Do you think I would cause you any pain whatsoever?'

'I don't know what to think, Ashok,' she confessed freely. 'Yesterday, when you showed up here, I was beyond the moon. I had hopes. Sure, I could not see the future with any clarity, but it seemed, after a long time of being alone, that I had finally found somebody. Now I am confused again. If you have to think so much about introducing me to your relative, then what about your family? Are you going to hide me from them forever? Visit whenever your official tours allow and have a few nights together?'

'She is my family.'

'She is your father's sister.'

'Which makes her my family. Anyway, if you feel so strongly about it, I shall pick you up at ten tomorrow. We will all go shopping. Happy?'

'No, I am not.'

Suddenly she found herself crowded against the kitchen sink. Ashok pulled her into his arms and brought his mouth down on hers. She struggled furiously for a second and then suddenly went soft. Could she ever resist him? As the kiss deepened, she felt sadness swell within her, but she knew not why. Tears prickled her eyes.

'Oh, darling, I hate to see you cry. Please don't cry. Everything will be all right, I promise you,' Ashok murmured over her head.

'How? Tell me—how? We live too far apart, Ashok. This can never work, not this way at least.' Tears fell faster now. 'I hate to think of us apart,' she wailed.

'We will be together,' Ashok vowed. 'Now, dry your tears and get some sleep. I want you to look your best when you meet my aunt.'

As he made for the door, Annie asked, in spite of herself, 'But won't you stay?'

'I have to go, Annie. I can spare a few hours first thing in the morning tomorrow, but I really do have to attend the afternoon session.'

'Okay, goodnight then.'

'Goodnight, Annie. See you tomorrow.' Ashok strode out of the door.

CHAPTER 19

Ashok's aunt was a sweet plump lady of about sixty. She wore a sari and had wrapped herself up securely in an overcoat and a shawl.

'I don't trust the weather at all,' she declared. 'What if I catch a cold? I don't want to die in this foreign land.'

'Tai, nobody is going to die. It is not that cold even,' Ashok mildly protested. They had arrived to pick up Annie from her house; it was a bright morning, though there was a nip in the air. Annie came out as the rented car pulled up in front of her gate. She was wearing a pair of faded jeans and a dark-grey full-sleeved T-shirt. Her hair was tied back with a green scarf.

'Hello, Annie,' Ashok said. He sounded a bit stiff, but he smiled at her and extended his hand. Not knowing what was expected of her, Annie took it in a handshake of sorts.

'Hello,' she said in a steady voice even though she was unsure inside. She wanted Ashok's family to like her, and for all practical purposes, this was the first time she was meeting a member of the clan. She felt positively nervous.

'This is my aunt, Neli Singh. Tai, this is my friend I told you about. Her name is Annie. She will help you shop today.'

'Hello, child. I am so glad that you can help.' Neli smiled at her, not unkindly.

'Think nothing of that, Neli,' Annie said as she climbed into the car after her. She missed Neli's surprised look and Ashok's uncomfortable one as she did so.

Ashok gave instructions to the chauffer where to take them so they can do some shopping. Annie waved at Ashok and then sat back, turning to look at Neli. She looked kind and gentle, and she relaxed a bit. Maybe it wouldn't be so bad after all. She even felt a little ashamed at her outburst the night before; it seemed now that Ashok had not meant to hide her after all. He was just as unsure as she was about his family.

'So, Neli, how do you like Miami so far?' she asked now in her most friendly voice, but to her consternation, Ashok's aunt frowned.

'You might call me Auntie, dear,' Neli said in a coolly polite voice.

Annie was taken aback but decided not to press a point. It meant that she was being accepted on some level, she reasoned to herself.

They left the car, leaving instructions to pick them up after a couple of hours when they would have lunch. Annie and Neli explored the various curio shops and some clothes shops, where Neli picked up a few things to take back home.

'Presents, you understand. They will all expect something brought back from abroad,' she explained to Annie as she rummaged through the little souvenirs piled up on trays on roadside stalls.

'But, Auntie, you can get much better things from those shops out there,' Annie tried to say, but she was brushed aside with a quick sweeping gesture of her beringed hand.

'No, no, they are very expensive. These will do fine,' she said, picking up a few more of the tiny statues of Liberty. Annie gave up. She simply trailed behind Neli after that as she darted from one shop to the other; Ashok had discreetly deserted them, murmuring something about 'urgent work', and she was all on her own in this.

'I am finished. Now, we have lunch,' Neli announced about an hour later, much to Annie's relief. She felt rather famished herself, having skipped breakfast that morning. She had been too tense to eat then, but now her stomach positively rumbled.

'Shall we find a place to eat then?' she asked. She reckoned it was easier to let Neli decide, but she was shaking her head.

'No, no. Ashok will come and pick us up. He phoned me just now.'

Sure enough, Ashok appeared; the chauffer had picked him up after his meeting. They all went to a restaurant on the ground floor of a five-star hotel.

'This is where my conference is being held, so it will be convenient for me,' Ashok explained. 'Later, the car can drop you off,' he told his aunt.

They ordered their food. Neli wanted to taste seafood, so they had giant broiled lobsters for the main course and a green salad to accompany it. Annie expected Ashok to ask for the wine menu, but he said he would have water instead. Annie concurred even though she thought white wine would bring out the taste of the lobsters better.

As they ate, they conversed over a number of subjects; it seemed that Neli was visiting the States for the first time, and she shared her experiences with Ashok, supplying anecdotes that had Annie laughing out loud. His anecdotes about Sunil, his cousin and Neli's son, brought an indulgent smile to his aunt's lips.

'Go on, you!' she admonished. 'Don't make fun of your little brother. Besides, Annie must be bored with us talking only about ourselves.' She turned to Annie.

'Now, tell me about yourself,' she said. 'What about your children—are they going to college too?'

Annie felt uncomfortable. 'Well, I . . .' she started. Sensing her discomfiture, Ashok hastily intervened.

'Tai, I am sure Annie has much better things to discuss than her family right now.'

'No. No, it's okay,' Annie assured him. It was not. They had never discussed her children before; she had no idea about Ashok's feelings about children, hers or anybody else's. But it was not something that could be avoided forever, and she decided now was as good a time as any other. Turning to Ashok's aunt, she took a deep breath and said, 'I have four children. My firstborn stays in Trinidad, where he is in banking and finance. The second child is a daughter, who is a nurse, and the third one also works for a bank. The youngest one is married and lives and works in North Carolina. He majored in sports and recreation.'

'Oh. That's nice. All studying and working and everything. Don't you live with your husband?'

'Tai, try this salad with the apple cider. It will bring a nice tang into your mouth,' Ashok smoothly interjected. Annie stole a glance at his face. He looked at his aunt impassively, no signs betraying his feelings about this revelation. Annie felt a bit peeved, which only proved her perverseness. But she would have liked it better if Ashok had shown some kind of reaction to his aunt's questions. Even a negative one would mean that he cared enough. But maybe he didn't, she thought to herself.

'I hate apple cider. Too sour,' Neli retorted. Turning to Annie, she pressed on. 'What does your husband do?'

'I am divorced,' Annie said with a smile. She did not like the prying, but she wanted to be polite. This was Ashok's aunt, and she loved him.

'Divorced? Oh my. So sad. Are you all alone now?' Neli asked.

Annie wanted to answer, 'No, I have your nephew now,' but her eyes met Ashok's before she could open her mouth. He looked stricken. Besides, she could find no hint of malice in Neli's question; it seemed she genuinely wanted to know. So she answered, 'Not alone, no. I have friends. And my family keeps in touch with me.'

'Where are they living?' Neli wanted to know. But Ashok had had enough.

'Tai, you have to leave now. Sunil has arrived to pick you up. You can talk to Annie later. Come on, now. Sunil will be waiting.'

'Oh, but you said—' Neli protested as she stood up to gather her purse.

'Change of plans. Sunil called, and he is going to pick you up. Say goodbye to Annie, will you?'

As Ashok led his aunt towards the lobby, he did not look back. Annie felt absolutely out of her depth; she had no idea what to do. Was she expected to pick up the entire check for lunch? This place was way beyond her means; she was sure their lunch would cost more than her week's earnings. Maybe he wanted to drive home a point after last night?

But Ashok came back as she sat there wondering.

'Sorry about the entire episode,' he said as he sat down. 'My aunt can be a handful. I should have warned you.'

'No problem at all. Though her prying into my personal matters did make me a tad uncomfortable, I have to admit.'

'She did not mean to pry, Annie. Indian culture allows personal questions—it means that you are friendly.'

'I suppose I made a faux pas by calling her by her name?'

'You did that, yes. We do not address older people by their name. It is usually by a relation, aunt or uncle, or *bhai* or *bahen*, which means brother or sister, as the case may be.'

'I will remember from now on. I thought you would introduce me to your cousin though.'

'I will, some other time. I couldn't wait to see the back of my aunt now, so I let him pick her up at the lobby. I want you to myself for a little while more.' Ashok smiled and took a sip from his glass. Grimacing, he put it down immediately. 'Ugh! What is this vile stuff?'

'Tonic water.' Annie laughed. 'You wanted it, remember?'

'What I wanted was white wine, which I will get now.' Ashok caught the eye of a passing waiter and asked for the wine list. Then he turned back to Annie. 'I couldn't ask for alcohol in my aunt's presence. Now, could I?'

'Why not?' Annie's brows went up. 'Would she have minded? Is this one more of your Indian things?'

'I am not accustomed to drinking in the presence of elders,' Ashok said coolly. 'If that is my "Indian thing" to you, then so be it.'

The waiter brought the wine list. Annie waited until Ashok was finished with ordering, and then she said contritely, 'I am sorry. I meant no disrespect. But you are so different from me. I find it a wonder that we—'

'Love each other? It can happen, Annie. What does it matter, these small differences? The main thing is we want to be with each other. That's what counts.'

They finished their meal leisurely after that, talking and sharing. Ashok made her laugh, and she was sorry to see lunch come to an end. But he had a conference to attend, and they took leave of each other. Ashok said he would see her in the evening after he was done with his business.

CHAPTER 20

ANNIE TOOK A CAB HOME. She had some errands to run, so she let go of the cab near the supermarket and walked the remaining few blocks. As she walked, she thought about the day that she had spent with Ashok and his aunt. Did she like it? She was a little dazed by the strangeness of it all. This was the first time she had met an Indian who actually was a current resident of the place; her experiences with the people when she visited the country as a tourist had not prepared her for this. With Ashok, she often forgot where he came from, but now it occurred to her that she knew not much about him, including his religious beliefs, his customs, and his family, extended or otherwise. But seeing Ashok with his aunt, the easy affection they shared, suddenly made her long for her parents. She resolved to call them once she finished picking up her groceries.

As she looked for supplies on the shelves, she had an idea to cook dinner for Ashok that evening. He would love that, and she would love cooking for him. She didn't know much in the culinary field, but she wanted to make him one Indian dish at least. How hard could that be? She rummaged in the Indian section with suddenly enthused determination, picking up herbs and spices before going to the checkout counter with her purchases.

A couple of hours later, she was close to tears; nothing had gone according to plan. She had overcooked the rice; it resembled a mushy gel-like glob that was singularly unappetizing. The chicken curry did not take off well either; it had no resemblance to the yellow-red sumptuous dish she had had in India. Her chicken looked burnt and underdone alternately, with the curry looking like a dark paste. Heaven knew how she managed to achieve that colour; she certainly did nothing for it to look as hideous as that. To make matters worse, she had no time to wash her hair. She was supposed to wash her hair today; it clung to her head like limp noodles, made worse by the heat of the kitchen. She had no idea what to do—to start cooking again or rush to the bathroom for a quick shower before Ashok arrived.

The bathroom won. There was no way she was going to let Ashok look at her the way she was now; she simply had to get ready fast. She poured shampoo on her hair and scrubbed furiously, refusing to let the tears fall. After her shower, she picked up a two-toned loose dress in light blue and dove grey. She dragged a comb through her wet hair and put some moisturizer on her face. There was no time for anything else as that was precisely when the doorbell rang.

'Hi, am I late?' Ashok came in and pulled her into his arms. He had discarded his jacket, and his shirt was open at the neck, giving a glimpse of his tan skin. He lifted his head and sniffed. 'Is that chicken?' he asked.

Annie burst into tears. She couldn't help it; all the frustration and fear came wailing out of her.

Ashok was mortified. 'Annie, Annie, I am so sorry. Don't cry, darling, please don't. What is the matter, baby? Hush, now, shhh,' he murmured, smoothing her wet hair.

'I cooked for you, but the rice got lumpy, and the chicken burned, and now you are going to laugh at me, and I am such a failure I want to die,' Annie finished in a rush between anguished hiccups.

'Hey, hey, come on now, hush.' Ashok carried her to the couch and sat her on his lap. 'It doesn't matter. What does ruined chicken matter? You wanted to cook for me. That is so sweet, Annie.'

'But I made such a mess! Everybody knows how to cook—all the women you have known—and I am so hopeless!' Tears welled up again in her eyes.

'Listen to me.' Ashok took her face in both his hands. 'All the women I have known before you, they all wanted to have a good time with me.' He made a face. 'To be fair to them, I wanted that of them too. Nobody ever wanted to cook for me, and I couldn't care less. But you—you are different. You are special. I am so happy, Annie. You made me so happy right now, you have no idea.'

'Why?' Annie asked. She was not being coy; she really wanted to know.

Ashok laughed in delight. 'Because you cared enough! Don't you see what that means to me?'

Annie wiped her cheeks with the back of her palm; she suddenly became aware of how she must look, her face red and blotched and wriggled to get away. Ashok tightened his hold.

'Where are you going?' he asked.

'I look a fright,' Annie mumbled, ashamed of herself anew. He must be thinking she was a complete idiot; she was sure of it.

'You look beautiful. I love the way you smell, so fresh and like a . . . a flower.' He bent his head to kiss her, breathless, as dinner was the last thing on his mind at that moment. He picked her up and took her to the bedroom.

Much later, Annie lifted her head from where it lay on Ashok's chest. 'We never did get around to dinner.'

'Hmmm. How would you like pizza?'

'I'd love that.' Annie grabbed her phone from the bedside table and dialled the number while Ashok disappeared into the bathroom. She could hear the shower running as she ordered.

'I ordered a large pepperoni. I hope you don't mind,' she said as he came out of the bathroom.

'I like pepperoni, thank you.'

Annie was a little sorry to see him pull on his trousers over his shorts and tuck the ends in; the thought of sharing pizza from a box wearing nothing but a robe was such a delicious, intimate thought. But maybe he wasn't ready for that yet. In any case, he had to go back. A cloud passed over her thoughts.

'What is it?' Ashok was quick to notice her change in mood.

'Nothing.'

'Something is bothering you.' The bed dipped as he sat down. 'Tell me about it.'

Annie looked up, her eyes troubled. 'I was thinking right now, you have to leave.'

'Well, I have a presentation tomorrow . . .'

'No, I meant you have to leave for home. Soon your visit here will be over.'

'Well, yes.' Ashok looked at her quizzically.

'Ashok, where do you think we are going? This can't get us far enough, can it?' Annie felt miserable that she had brought the topic up. He would leave her now; she was sure of that. Nobody wanted a nag for a lover.

'I am not sure, Annie,' Ashok said sombrely. 'I have never done this before. I am taking it as it comes and making my way along with it. But I can promise you this: what I feel for you is not fleeting.'

'People do get attracted to exotic affairs and . . .' Annie began.

'I cannot of course say for you,' Ashok said coolly, 'but I can assure you, to me, it is much more than some exotic affair. I love you.'

'How can you say—no, even think of—such a thing?' Annie could feel her anger rise. 'I have loved you from the very first day I saw you, maybe even before that. If it was a holiday romance, then I would not have suffered the way I have since I left India . . .' Tears choked her voice, but they were tears of outrage.

Ashok looked at her for a moment, amazed, and then a wide smile spread over his face. 'So you love me, huh?' he said in a deep voice. 'And from the very first moment you saw me?'

'There is no reason to gloat.' Annie scrubbed her eyes with the back of her hands, rather like a child.

'Oh, but I can't help it. Here I was, torturing myself, imagining that maybe I was nothing but a piece of exotic white chocolate to you . . .'

Annie giggled suddenly. 'White chocolate? God, how corny!'

'Well, what can I say? I am no poet. But the point here is I beat myself up with doubts and thought that I was making a fool of myself a thousand times before I showed up at your door. And now I learn that you have loved me all this time. I think that calls for a serious bout of gloating.'

'So you took a risk?' Annie smirked.

'And how!' Ashok said fervently. 'This was the most risky venture in my life. If you hadn't loved me, then where would I be? All my efforts—I had to pull some serious strings to be included in this conference—would have been in vain. Splashed down the drain.'

'Ummm . . . you have pale skin . . .' Annie giggled some more. 'Milk chocolate would be more like it. I do like milk chocolate . . .'

'Annie!' Ashok admonished her.

'Okay. Yes,' Annie said soberly. 'But now that you are here, what do we do about it? I mean, now what? A few days of romancing, and then we go our own ways and back to our old days?'

'Why can't we have the good days first and think about the rest later? You know, kind of take it as it comes along?'

'Because at the end of it all, it is going to hurt like hell. I could barely keep up when I thought I had left you behind, put thousands of kilometres between us, but now that you are here, right at my doorstep, in my bed, invading my most private space, I don't think I can cope with that. When you go away, and you will, unless you have plans to settle here permanently, how do you think it will be for me?'

'Why are you bringing all this up now?' Ashok protested.

'Somebody has to be the responsible one in this relationship, Ashok, and I have this suspicion it is going to be me.'

'Being responsible doesn't mean being a killjoy.'

There was a stunned silence after that. Then both of them spoke at once.

'I am sorry,' Ashok started, while Annie said, 'If you think that of me, I suggest we end this right now.'

'I said I am sorry,' Ashok said. 'I didn't mean it. It just came out wrong.'

'Maybe. But maybe you did mean it. I . . . I need to think about it. Give me some time, Ashok.'

'We don't have the luxury of time, Annie. I want the period of my stay to matter. To you and to me.'

'Just this night then. Can you give me this night?'

Something in the way she spoke told Ashok that his protests would not change the situation. He looked at Annie for a long moment and then simply nodded and left.

'This is not the end. I shall be back,' he said. Then he was gone.

Annie was left standing in the middle of the room, clutching her robe, staring into nothingness. *What just went wrong?* she thought. They were supposed to have dinner and make love and then . . .

The doorbell rang. Annie came out of her stupor and raced to the door, her heart in her mouth. But it was the pizza deliveryman. Numbly, she paid for it and took the box in her hands, then stood for some time, unsure what to do with it. Slowly she went to the counter and set the box down, then sat on the stool, her head in her arms, for a long time. Life had become complicated. A simple holiday in the tropics was not supposed to bring so much—she lifted her head—so much what? Passion? Joy? Yes, there was uncertainty about the future; she was not even sure this was going to last. But on the other hand, when was the last time she had felt so alive? Annie thought about her life of the past few years carefully. She had gone through the motions of living, but had she ever lived? Her first two relationships had promised a future, but they had ended in disaster. Ashok was yet to speak about any long-term commitment, but at least he was honest. And he was right. She was ruining the present for her fear of the future. What did that mean anyway? What the future was to her at some time was now the past. And that past was not something that brought very many happy moments.

She looked around her living room with wonder as if she were seeing it for the first time. 'I have to call him,' she said to herself. 'I made a mess. I have to clean it up.'

But calling him was no easy task. Annie's inherent reticent nature, coupled with what she now knew about his family, made the task difficult enough. 'I shall call him tomorrow morning,' she decided. 'It is too late to call now.'

And indeed it was. Checking the tiny silver watch on her wrist, she saw it was almost midnight. She had been sitting there on the counter stool for a good couple of hours. The pizza was cold and soggy; she put it in the garbage. Hunting around in the fridge, she came up with a box of cheese. She knew there was a tin of crackers somewhere, and sure enough, looking around in the kitchen cabinets, she found them. She had crackers and cheese, washing it down with some red wine before finally turning off the lamps and going to bed.

CHAPTER 21

I T WAS NOT QUITE DAWN when Annie woke up the next day. She lay in bed for some time, remembering last evening, her breathing heavy with regret. She now saw quite clearly that she had been a royal pain in the neck. She resolved to make things better. With that note, she jumped out of bed, put on her tracksuit, tied up her hair in a matching baby-pink scrunchy, and put on her running shoes. She was going to turn over a new leaf. And it started now.

Picking up her water bottle from the kitchen table, she was on her way.

An hour and a half later, Annie was doubled up on the sidewalk in front of her home, her breathing coming in gasps as her tortured lungs tried to cope with this unaccustomed exercise. There was a stitch on her left side, and her feet hurt. In fact, her whole body hurt. She felt such a fool for trying out something so drastic; she was not even sure she could make it up the short walk to her doorstep. Maybe she would just lay down here and die . . .

'Annie. Good morning.'

It was Ashok. Annie shut her eyes in embarrassment; just her luck to be at her worst when he came to see her! When would she ever learn? She tried to smile at him, but all she could do was sort of open and close her mouth in an excellent imitation of a fish, her uncooperative lungs still intent on drawing the next breath. Ashok's eyes went around in concern.

'Are you okay?' He bent down to peer at her face while she held on to her knees in a death grip, her face looking down at the pavement. She managed to nod her head. She was okay. Or she would be, in maybe another hour, if he just went away now.

Ashok did not say another word. Instead, he picked her up as if she weighed nothing and marched towards her door. Annie squirmed in his arms, ready to die of embarrassment; the neighbours must have been having an eyeful.

'Stop wriggling,' Ashok said sternly.

'I am not,' Annie rasped.

'She can talk,' Ashok marvelled as he shifted her in his arms and delved his hand in her pocket for the key.

Annie tried to slap his hand away. 'Under the doormat.'

Ashok set her gently on the ground and took the key from under the mat. He turned it in and opened the door and ushered her in—as if he owned the place, Annie thought resentfully. But she felt better instantly as Ashok put on the air conditioner immediately. Annie sank into the couch gratefully as Ashok went straight to the kitchen. She could hear the sound of water running from the tap. Presently, he came back, a wet towel in his hands. Sitting beside her, he pressed it to her temple; it felt blissful. Annie sighed. Her shoulders, back, neck, thighs, legs, and feet hurt.

'Now, tell me,' Ashok said, putting the wet cloth down on the floor (*Typical*, Annie thought), 'what do you think you were doing out there?'

'What did it look like I was doing? I was running.'

'Oh. I thought you were training for the army,' Ashok said with a grave face. 'Or maybe the mob was after you and you were running for your life.'

'Very funny. You have to stay in shape, you know. It is important,' Annie retorted.

'Of course,' Ashok agreed instantly with a straight face. Annie peered suspiciously into his face but found no sarcasm there. She relaxed a little.

'Now, I am going to make coffee while you finish catching your breath.' Ashok started off for the kitchen again.

'What were you doing here at this hour anyway?' Annie asked, picking up the wet towel from the floor and wiping her arms and neck with it. She needed a shower. Heavens! Did she stink? She would die if she did.

'I thought I would come early, and then we would go out on a picnic. The day promises to be sunny. Even you cannot say no to that.'

'And what made you think that I would be sure to go with that?' Annie asked tartly.

'Come on, Annie. You know you would love that.' Ashok poked his head out of the kitchen. 'Besides, I was sure of you feeling bad about yesterday and was ready to use it shamelessly. To my advantage.'

'I do not feel bad about—' Annie began.

Ashok cut her off with, 'The kettle's boiled. Where do you keep your coffee?'

'Second shelf on the left. Along with the sugar. If you want cream, it is in the fridge.'

Annie got up at last from the sofa and went to the bathroom. She really needed to shower.

When she came out after a quarter of an hour, Ashok had a rack of toast and coffee ready on the breakfast counter. Annie slid into one stool and sniffed appreciatively.

'Mmm. It smells good. You are amazingly housebroken for an Indian bachelor,' she teased.

'What is that supposed to mean?'

'I just find Indian males to be a pampered lot. You people tend to be completely helpless when it comes to domesticity.'

'And you have lots of experience in Indian maleness, I suppose?' Ashok slid a plate of buttered toast over to her before taking a sip of his coffee. 'This coffee is good,' he said, looking surprised at his own endeavour.

'No, I am not.' Annie soberly agreed. 'What's more, the two males I have been within the past turned out to be complete jerks, so I suppose I stereotyped unfairly. I am sorry.'

'No need to be. It is okay. We are all guilty of that sometime or another,' Ashok said easily. 'Now, finish your toast and get ready. We are going out.'

'We are?'

'Mm-hm. The day is too beautiful to be indoors. I want you to take me to the beach.'

Half an hour later, they were out of the house. Ashok had brought a car, which was rented, he said. Since he was not comfortable with the left-hand driving, Annie took the wheel. Soon, they left the township behind and headed for the beach.

It was crowded, as usual. Annie grimaced, but Ashok was thrilled to be there.

'I have only seen them in photographs. I thought the colour of the water was Photoshopped for effect, but it is not. It is real,' he marvelled.

Annie smiled at his enthusiasm as she rolled out the mat on the sand and set the basket on it. She took off her shirt; she was wearing a two-piece bikini in shades of aqua. It was her favourite bathing suit, and she knew she looked good in it. She sat down on the towel and looked up at Ashok. 'You'd better put on lots of sun cream, or the sun can burn you,' she started to say but then stopped at the look on his face. He stared at her, his jaw slack and eyes riveted, fascinated.

'I have never seen you in a bikini.' He swallowed.

Annie smiled inwardly. 'Of course you haven't,' she said. 'We have never been to any beach before now.'

He dropped down beside her on the towel. 'Do you need lotion rubbed on your back?' he asked eagerly.

Annie laughed. 'No! Why do you ask?'

Ashok shrugged. 'Well, I suppose that is what is expected in a situation like this. One has to offer to rub lotion on the back. I have read it in books.' He grinned.

'You are naughty. Come on, the water is wonderful.' Annie got up and ran with light steps to the sea. It was true. The water was indeed wonderful. She loved the water. She had always loved the sea, in fact. One of the incentives of living in Miami was the sea; it never ceased to fascinate her.

'Come on! What are you waiting for?' she called out now. But Ashok shook his head.

'I am not sure I can last out there,' he called back. 'I'd rather stay here on the sand and look at you.'

Annie laughed again and swam out deeper with strong laps. She then turned and floated on her back, letting the gently swelling water relax her.

Suddenly she was pulled under by a pair of hands. She came up spluttering, brushing wet hair out of her face. Ashok laughed down at her.

'What did you do that for?' Annie spat saltwater from her mouth. 'I thought you were not comfortable in the sea?'

'Got you, didn't I?' Ashok grinned before swimming back towards the shore.

They swam, lay in the sand, and then swam some more before heading back. They had worked up a healthy appetite with their exercise and had freshly caught fish at the wharf. By the time they headed back towards her house, the sun was almost down.

CHAPTER 22

LATER THAT NIGHT, THEY LAY in bed. Ashok held her close, his hands absently smoothing her hair in a gesture so tender it brought tears to her eyes. Earlier too, their lovemaking had a sweet quality that was never before. Annie had felt particularly cherished as he made gentle love to her, taking his time to be with her every step of the way, never leaving her behind. Only when he was sure of her pleasure did he take his own. Annie had never experienced anything like this before.

She sighed and stirred a little, but his hold only tightened. Annie made a sound of protest.

'Sorry,' Ashok said and made to move away from her, but she laid his head on her shoulder and settled herself more comfortably. A cool breeze wafted in from the sea, bringing with it an aroma of tropical flowers and the mixed odour of the Miami nightlife. The room was dark; there was no moon tonight.

Annie had never felt so content in her life.

'Well, I really must go. It is time,' Ashok murmured.

'Do you have to?' Annie protested.

Ashok looked down at her in the darkness. Annie could feel his glance even in the darkness. 'You know I have to, Annie.' There was a tinge of regret in his voice.

'You are right.' Annie removed his hand from her shoulder and sat up. She leaned over and switched on the bedside lamp before leaning further down and picking up her dress from the floor. She wriggled into it and swung her feet on the ground. Looking back at Ashok, still reclined on the bed, she smiled.

'Fancy a drink? You know, one for the road?'

But Ashok wasn't smiling. He averted his eyes and got out of bed. His shorts lay on the chair at the other end of the room, where he had discarded them. He padded over to them, quite unabashed in his nudity, and put them on before looking around for his trousers.

'Ashok? Is anything wrong?'

He put on his shirt before turning around to face Annie, who waited in an agony of suspense.

'I have to leave, Annie.'

She frowned in puzzlement. 'Sure. I know that.'

'I mean, I have to leave for India.'

'Oh. When?'

'Tomorrow.' Ashok looked at his watch. 'Technically, today. My plane leaves at nine in the morning. I go to New York and then take the plane for Delhi from there.'

Annie's heart sank to her feet. It was like before, again. Only, this time he was leaving instead of her. And this time it was far worse than last time. She knew now that life would be impossible without him. He had implanted himself firmly inside her heart, and she did not know how to pluck him out and go on. Not this time.

She stared at him, speechless. Emotions bubbled inside her, but not one word came out of her lips. She just stood there in the middle of the room and looked at him, helpless in her misery.

Ashok came forward swiftly, seeing the stricken look in her face. 'Annie, don't be like that.' He took her in his arms. 'I swear . . .'

Annie came out of her stupor with a shudder. She stepped back from his arms, looking up at him, her lovely eyes flashing in anger. She was livid.

'What? You swear what? Hmm? Do you swear that you will love me to the end of the time, huh?'

'Of course I do.' Ashok was taken aback at her anger.

'Oh, really? And how do you plan to do that? By being halfway around the world? Exactly how do you propose that we love each other? Tell me that. Or do you plan to have a long-distance relationship based on great sex, seeing only when you can sneak away from relatives for a convenient conference? Tell me, Ashok, what if your company had not approved your coming here? What would you have done? Do you propose that we be at the mercy of your official policies and doles?'

'You are blowing this out of proportion, Annie,' Ashok tried to reason, but she was too angry to stop.

'I am not blowing this out of proportion. My heart broke when I had to leave you behind. I had started to pick up the pieces when you showed up here and promised me the sun, all the while not even mentioning how long you were going to stay when you were due to leave.'

'You never asked,' Ashok protested. 'You knew I had to go back home after the conference ended.'

'Why should I ask? Why wouldn't you tell me? And now you suddenly say that you are leaving in a few hours, and I don't know if I will ever see you again . . .' To her horror, Annie was bawling her eyes out.

Ashok moved swiftly to her, took her in his arms, and held her tightly. Annie returned the hug, weeping inconsolably. She felt her heart break in a thousand pieces; she could almost hear the shattering sound. She knew she would never recover from this.

'Shhh. Hush now. You will make yourself sick,' Ashok crooned softly. He gently led her to the bed and sat her down. He squatted on the floor before her so that he was eye to eye with her.

'Now, listen carefully,' he said softly, holding both her hands in his. 'I have to go back tomorrow. I am sorry that I did not prepare you for this, but I just wanted this to go on without the reminder of our parting, you know?' Annie nodded. She understood. That was why she too had avoided asking about his return date. She had not wanted to think about that. Their happiness together was too precious.

'I promise you, we will be together.' As Annie lifted her head in surprised denial, he put a finger on her lips. 'Hush. I promise you, and I always keep my promise. Remember that. We shall be together. I love you.' He paused. He sighed and picked up her limp hand and lightly touched the inside of her wrist with his lips. Even now, amidst all the misery, Annie's pulse jumped at the light touch. But that only made it clear that she was going to grieve terribly.

Slowly she extracted herself from his embrace, stepping back when he made to take her into his arms again. She wanted to put some distance between them, or she would never be free of him. It was her survival instinct kicking in, she recognized at some vague level, but pushed it to the back of her mind. There were other important things to be taken care now, more pressing issues than psychoanalysing herself.

'I don't think that would be a good idea, Ashok,' she slowly said. Ashok made as if to protest, but she shook her head. 'Please, allow me to speak.' She took a deep breath. 'I don't think we should see each other at all.'

Ashok made a movement of protest.

'No, listen to me, please. This—this on-and-off relationship will kill me. I know it will.'

'Now you are being overly dramatic,' he said.

'I am not. I have gone through so much, Ashok. I have just picked up the pieces and moved on. Every time, I have just concentrated on putting one foot ahead of another till I have pushed myself to be upright once more. But with you . . .' She choked, unable to carry on. She swallowed and then lifted her eyes to Ashok. 'Just leave, Ashok. I think you should leave. Now.'

'I will not leave you like this,' Ashok protested. 'And you are wrong. We do have a future together. Just give it some time. I shall figure this out. I promise.'

'There is nothing to figure out,' Annie almost screamed. 'Don't you see? This is it. This is all we can get. This is the best we can do. Now, please leave.'

Ashok stood in the middle of the room, helpless.

'Just go,' Annie whispered, turning away from him. She stood like that for a long time, dreading and expecting him to come and take her into his arms. If he did—

She turned around. There was nobody in the room. He had left. Annie couldn't believe that he was not there. She ran into the living room; maybe he was on the front porch? But the front porch was in darkness. She came back into the house, closing the front door after her. The house felt cold, as if all the warmth had been sucked out along with his departure.

How could he leave like that?

Annie thought of calling him back but pulled herself back at the last instant. Her dignity was something she could not let go of, not for anybody—not even for him. She simply had to learn to live without him. She had done it before, and she would do it again.

Only this time she was not sure she could make it.

CHAPTER 23

ANNIE WENT TO NEW YORK the next week. She had a meeting with a client who wanted to meet face to face before he gave her the job of putting together an incentive group for his firm on board one of the largest cruise ships out of Miami. She didn't mind as it would give her an opportunity to see her son Hank, who was going to be in New York at the same time. As she boarded the plane, she felt a rush of anticipation at the thought of seeing Hank. He was her firstborn, and it was more than a few months since she had seen him—since last Christmas, as a matter of fact.

The meeting with the client was to take place in his home office, where Annie was to meet him. Afterwards, she would have dinner with Hank before taking the evening flight home. She came out of the airport and got herself a cab, giving the address to the driver.

New York seemed congested and dingy after the sunshine and sea of Miami. Annie felt it every time she visited New York. But today it seemed worse than ever. Maybe it was the busy traffic or the endless sea of black-clad people rushing on streets, but she felt depressed just looking out of the window. She gave up after some time and simply closed her eyes; it had been early when she got up to get ready for the flight.

The cab came to a stop in front of a huge apartment building—the type with glass and shining chrome and a uniformed man at the door. She went in after the owner buzzed her in and was told to go up the elevator to the top floor. The elevator opened right into the living room of the apartment. She stepped on to the lush grey carpet, clutching her folder and purse in a death grip. She had never been to such an opulent setting before—not on her job anyway— and felt just a little bit out of her depth.

'Hello, you must be Annie,' a deep, husky voice greeted her. A tall man in his mid fifties came forward, extending his hand. His hair was grey at the temples, giving him a distinguished look, and his eyes crinkled when he smiled. Annie liked him on sight and felt herself relax.

'Hello. You must be Gerard Howard.'

'Guilty as charged. Come on in. We can begin in my office.' He led her through one of the doors that opened off the large living area. The office was ultra-modern, matching the decor of the rest of the place. There were a couple of state-of-the-art computer systems and a couple of sleek desks, but a large black chrome secretariat table dominated the room. Annie hovered on the threshold, a little bit awed by the sheer opulence of it all.

'Please, Annie, come on in. May I call you Annie?'

'Yes, of course. Uh, Mr Howard . . .'

'Gerard, please. Mr Howard sounds so old, don't you think? Something out of a fifties movie.'

Annie laughed; she was disarmed by his charm.

'Okay, Gerard then. I thought we might establish the primary preparations before we move into the major things.'

'Absolutely. Just tell me what you need, and we can start from there. Here, you can use this computer. It is linked to mine.'

Annie settled in front of one of the computers that Gerard indicated and logged in. 'Right. I shall need the figures, names, special amenities, how many conference rooms needed, total numbers of cabins . . .' Annie went on.

They worked in synch for the next couple of hours. Then Gerard dropped his pen and leaned back in his chair, rubbing his eyes.

'God, I am famished. Do you fancy lunch?'

'I am not really hungry. I would rather finish this off,' Annie replied, her eyes on the numbers on the screen. 'Why don't you get something, and I can have a sandwich, maybe.' She looked up. 'That is if it is not too much trouble.'

'No trouble at all. Double egg and tuna do for you?'

'Thank you. That would be lovely.'

It was almost evening when Annie finished her job. She had eaten the sandwich along with a glass of iced tea that Gerard had provided thoughtfully, but she was not aware that she was actually hungry till that moment. Now, as she looked up from the screen, passing her hand tiredly over her eyes, she was startled to see Gerard sitting still at his desk, his eyes on her. Suddenly she felt discomfited. 'Gosh, I had no idea it was so late,' she gushed nervously. 'I think we are done for the day though. I have all that I need here. I shall mail you the finished version by the end of the week.' She started to gather up her things. 'I shall leave now.'

Gerard stood up politely as she got up from her chair. 'Would you like to have dinner?' he asked gently.

'What? No. No, thank you. I shall just leave now.'

'You did not eat properly at lunch. You must be hungry,' Gerard observed mildly, but Annie sensed the steel behind his polite demeanour.

'I am,' she replied evenly, 'and I will have dinner. With my son who is meeting me in'—she checked her watch—'another twenty minutes. But thank you for the offer.'

'Okay,' Gerard said easily. 'Rain check then.'

'Absolutely.' Annie took her leave at last.

As she rode down the elevator, she thought about what had happened just then. She was not unaware of the male appreciation in Gerard's eyes. He was attracted to her, she mused thoughtfully, her brows furrowing in concentration. Gerard Howard was handsome, successful, and a gentleman. Annie was aware that many women would be very glad to be in her shoes right now. Yet all she felt about the whole situation was faint discomfort with a hint of annoyance. Was she going to be ruined for all the men for the rest of her life? She felt a surge of resentment at Ashok; no doubt he was safe and sound in the midst of his family while she pined for him, and she was unable to appreciate a good potential when she saw one! Well, bully for him. She would show him that she was quite capable of going on with her life on her own! She needed nobody.

'Hank!' Annie's face creased into a smile as soon as she spotted her eldest come towards her in the restaurant.

'Mom.' Hank bent down and kissed her cheek. 'You look wonderful.'

'Oh, hush. I know how I look. Let me look at you.' Annie hugged Hank and then held him away to look at him. 'You look great too. Now come on, let's eat. I am hungry. I didn't have a proper lunch, and I have a plane to catch later.'

They were shown to their table once inside. 'So tell me, what have you been doing these days?' Hank asked after they had ordered.

'Well, I travelled,' Annie began.

'Ah, yes. India. How was it? Was it very hot?' Hank asked.

For a moment, Annie hesitated. She wanted to confess about Ashok, but then she caught herself just in time. What was there to say? She had thought she had found her soulmate, but she had made a fool of herself. Even if he loved her, it was an impossible situation. There was nothing to say; Hank wouldn't understand.

'It was not very hot there,' she said instead. 'In fact, it was quite pleasant, seeing that it was winter there.'

They chatted while they ate. Hank wanted to know about her trip; she wanted to know about Hank's job, his wife, and the two girls.

'I had an offer today—to have dinner. It was my new client,' Annie confided.

'Really? What's he like?'

'Handsome. In his mid fifties, wealthy. I should know. I am handling his accounts.' She laughed.

'So why are you here?' Hank asked.

'Because I wanted to see my son, who has been neglecting his old mother for several months now,' Annie teased.

'Oh, come on, Mom! You are not too old. In fact, you should have someone with you—you know, a partner or something. You should not be alone at your age.'

'I am happy the way I am,' Annie said. She thought fleetingly of Ashok but then ruthlessly stuffed it back. He was gone, and there was no point in crying for the gone. 'I still remember what happened last time I tried.'

'Zack was not very nice to you,' Hank acknowledged. 'Why don't you take up this dude's offer? You know this client?'

'No!' Annie protested, laughing. 'I never allow business and pleasure to mix.'

Hank shrugged. 'Your loss, I think.'

'I think I have brought you up better than that,' Annie rebuked.

Soon it was time for her to leave. Hank promised to call her more often before he dropped her off at the airport. As she waited to board, her thoughts went back to what Hank had said earlier. She could have taken up Gerard's offer to have dinner; it was impossible to mistake the appreciation in his eyes. He was interested all right. But she did not feel anything for him—not even a spark.

Maybe she was destined to live alone for the rest of her life, she thought to herself. 'In that case, I have to accept it with good grace,' she told herself.

CHAPTER 24

ASHOK RANG LATER THAT WEEK. She had just settled down with a cup of chocolate, her comfort drink, after a particularly harrowing day. The living-room air conditioner had broken down, and it had taken a string of frantic calls and a couple of hours to fix it. By the time that was done, the living area was a mess of carbon, grease, and dirty rags. She cleaned everything up and then remembered that she had completely forgotten about the laundry.

Now, at last, with her chores done and dinner completed, she was curled up on the couch with her favourite cup and her favourite drink when the cell trilled. It was him!

She almost dropped the tiny handset, her fingers trembled so much, but she managed to flip it open and take the call.

'Hello?'

'Annie.'

Just hearing him say her name in that deep, sexy voice gave her goosebumps down her neck.

'Ashok. Hi,' she said in a shaky voice.

'What are you doing?' he wanted to know.

'Why?' Annie demanded.

Ashok laughed. 'I was missing this. Do you have to be so suspicious?'

'I am not suspicious. You make me sound as if I were paranoid or something,' Annie protested. And so the banter went back and forth, as if there were not more than three thousand kilometres between them.

After a quarter of an hour, Annie said, 'Please ring off now. Long distance calls will cost you a fortune.'

'I don't care,' Ashok said casually. 'I don't have much interest in anything else nowadays, so I am managing to put away quite a portion of my salary.'

'Even then, I feel guilty,' Annie pleaded.

'All right then. I will call you soon, Annie.'

'Yes, Ashok.'

'I love you, and I miss you very much. Please know that,' he said. And he rang off. Annie found herself smiling as she put the handset back.

She finished her drink and was just getting into bed when the phone rang again. Her heart missed a beat. Surely . . . but no, it was Becky this time.

'Hey, what is the matter with you?' Becky demanded to know in that no-nonsense manner of hers.

'Really? At this time of night?' Annie retorted.

'This is the only time I know we can talk in peace.'

Annie had to agree with that. 'Okay, shoot. What do you want to know?' she asked Becky, sliding in further under the covers.

'What are you even doing nowadays? I tried to call you at home, but your phone kept ringing. That was last week.'

'I had flown to New York on an assignment. Why didn't you try my cell?'

'I would have, but Pixie ate my handset.' Pixie was the new puppy. 'I had to buy myself a new set and then retrieve all my contacts.'

Annie laughed. 'You never have a dull moment, Becky.'

They chatted for a little while, and then Annie told her about Hank. 'I saw him this week when I was in New York.'

'And how is the strapping old man doing?'

Annie smiled, remembering how Hank and Becky would banter back and forth when he was growing up. She would call him her 'strapping old man', and he would call her his 'pretty little maid'.

'He is great. Advised me about my love life, so I think his is okay,' Annie joked.

'Have you told him about Ashok?' Becky asked soberly.

'No, I haven't. What is the point? It is not that anything is going to come out of this.'

'I don't know, girl. When he was here, you were on a different plane altogether. It was as if you were a completely different person. I have never seen you like this before.'

'I love him, Becky. I suspect I will always love him. But I also realize that it is quite impossible for us to be together. I don't want to get my children's hopes up and then dashed, much like mine has been.'

'What does Ashok say about all this?'

'He called,' Annie confessed.

'Really? When?'

'Earlier in the evening.' She found herself smiling; she slapped her mouth shut, though there was nobody in the room to see her.

'Hmmm. And how do you feel about it?'

'Oh, Becky . . .'

'I thought so. I think you are being too hasty, Annie. You have to give it some time and see what develops. Maybe there will be a way. Who knows?'

'I doubt it, but thanks all the same.'

They talked a bit more after that before saying goodnight to each other.

Ashok kept his word. He called her at least once a day for the next few months. Annie looked forward to those phone calls; they were the high point of her days, though she never initiated any. She was still wary of lowering her guard.

'I wish I were right in front of you now,' Ashok said one day. 'These phone calls only make my frustration starker.'

'Likewise,' said Annie.

'Tell you what. I shall get a new laptop. Then we can Skype.'

'That would be great.' Annie perked up.

Ashok did get a new laptop, and soon they were Skyping through the Net. Annie took care to put on her best face when she sat for the chat. They would talk for long minutes before she went to bed. This became a routine for them for the next couple of months.

'I will not be there tomorrow,' Ashok told her. 'I will be back on chat after a week.'

'Oh.' Annie tried to hide her disappointment. 'Why? Are you going somewhere?'

'My parents are coming to visit. They will be at my place for a week, so I will be busy with them.' Ashok looked rueful.

But Annie had a sinking feeling in her stomach. 'Why can't you chat for a few minutes even if they are there? Surely you can spare a few minutes?'

'You forget, this is daytime here, Annie. Mostly, I will be out with them, visiting places, my relatives, and so on. Besides, they don't know about you.'

'That is easily remedied. Tell them about me.'

But Ashok shook his head. 'I don't think they are ready yet. I will tell them when the time is right.'

'You do know how you sound, don't you, Ashok?' Annie hated the way the conversation was going, but she couldn't stop herself. 'You sound as if you are ashamed of me.'

'That is rubbish. We all have our own time and place about this. Have you told your children about me? I know you haven't. But I don't think you are ashamed of me, Annie. I simply assume that you will find the right time to open up about us.'

'You are right. But if any of them were here right now, I wouldn't stop chatting. I would not say I shall be away for a week.'

'Annie . . .' began Ashok, but she shook her head.

'Goodnight, Ashok. I am sleepy. See you in a week.' She snapped the laptop shut, her voice choking on the last few syllables. She felt her face warm up, and she was not sure whether she was angry or saddened. Probably it was a bit of both. How dare he treat her like this? So what if his parents were coming over? Surely he could have found some time for her. It was not asking for too much. She wiped angry tears from her eyes and stomped off to the bathroom, ignoring the ringing of the cell phone. She needed to have a shower.

Ashok tried to call her several times during the week, but Annie was too pissed off with him and refused to talk to him. Let him stew! She would show him that she had some backbone after all.

She went about her work, met clients, prepared trips, did her laundry, went to the store, cooked and cleaned, and nursed a bruised heart in the midst of it all. It was bearable during the times when she was busy, but when night came and she was alone in bed, she could not prevent heartache from returning with vengeance. She remembered how they had laughed and enjoyed the sun together, how he had held her in his arms. The memories of the feel of his hands and the smell of his skin threatened to overwhelm her in her moments of solitude. Sometimes she would put on the blue cotton dress she had bought from the Rajasthani shop and gaze at herself in the mirror. Then she would sigh and put it away in the closet before giving in to a flood of tears. She almost wished she had not met him; it would have spared her the pain she was going through now. But she knew that she would never have traded this for anything in the world. Ashok had shown her that life could bring so much joy and fun and caring. She felt she had not known life at all before she had met him.

CHAPTER 25

'**I** FEEL I HAVE LED A mundane, superficial existence till now,' she confessed to Becky during one of their phone conversations. Becky thought she was being foolish in handling the situation.

'You should not cut off communication altogether. That is stupid.'

'He doesn't love me enough. If he did, then he would be proud of me, not try to hide me from his parents.'

'The question is, do you love him enough? If you do, then you should grab whatever you get from him with both hands, or you stand the chance to lose him totally.'

Annie thought about that at length before picking up the phone. After dialling his number, she almost hung up but forced herself to wait—with bated breath—while it rang. It took some time before he answered, and she lost her courage before reminding herself that it was the middle of the night in India. Finally, he picked up the phone.

'Annie!'

'Hi,' Annie said in a subdued voice. 'Did I wake you up?'

'You did. But I am happy that you called, so that doesn't matter. God, it feels so good to hear your voice,' Ashok said.

'I am sorry. I behaved in a completely unreasonable way. I understand that . . .' Annie began, but Ashok cut her off.

'It doesn't matter. I was at my wit's end trying to contact you, but everything is going to be all right now. Can you come to Skype now?'

'What, now?' Annie laughed.

'Right now. I want to look at your face when we talk. Besides, my parents are safely asleep, so this is the best time to chat.'

Annie stubbornly smothered the feeling of being let down. 'Right, let's chat then.'

They Skyped for some time before Ashok suddenly yawned midsentence.

'I am so sorry.' Annie was immediately contrite. 'I woke you in the middle of the night. Please go back to sleep.'

'I shall call you before Skyping tomorrow,' Ashok promised. 'I am taking my parents to see my cousin in Agra and should be back by evening. Will that be all right?'

'Sure.' Annie brought down the lid of the laptop. She felt depressed. Ashok still had not told his parents about her. Maybe he never would. Maybe Annie would forever remain in the periphery of his life, an occasional partner whom he would take up with when convenient for him. She tried to reassure herself with the thoughts that he seemed genuinely happy to hear from her, but the feeling of being let down persisted.

She spent the rest of the day furiously cleaning her house until she had scrubbed it within an inch of its frames and the whole place gleamed. Then she fell into an exhausted sleep.

It rained the next day. The gloomy weather did nothing to cheer her up; she did not feel like going out in the windy weather even though she had to pick up groceries. She checked the fridge; there were some eggs and cheese. She would have to make do with those. Besides, Ashok might call any moment.

Sure enough, he called in a few minutes.

'Annie! How are you?'

'It is raining here, so not so good. I hate rain.'

'It is bright and sunny here,' Ashok remarked.

'So we are discussing weather now, are we? That is very British, I believe,' she said, tongue in cheek. Ashok laughed.

'Come to Skype,' he said and hung up.

Annie could see the familiar sofa in the background when she opened the video chat site. He was in his living room. He smiled when she connected.

'I have a surprise for you,' he said.

'Really? What is it? I love surprises,' Annie said with childlike pleasure.

'I hope you like this too,' Ashok said before turning his head to beckon somebody. An elderly face peeped over his shoulder. 'Annie, meet my mother. Mummy, this is Annie, my friend from the States.'

Annie was taken completely by surprise; it was all she could do to smile feebly and say hello in a whisper. She had not expected this in her wildest wishful dreams. She did not know what to do. God, was she even presentable? With great willpower, she resisted the urge to look down at herself. She was wearing a light sweater since the day was cold, and she was glad that the burnt sepia colour suited her. At least she was decently covered. She knew from experience that Indian women almost always shunned exposure of too much skin.

She was furious with Ashok for springing a surprise like this.

The face smiled back, even if a little uncertainly. 'Hello, Annie. I have heard about you from Ashok. I am glad that you were there when he went to America. He has told me how you helped him and his aunt, and I thank you for that.' The face went away.

'Friend?' Annie giggled. She felt a hysterical urge to laugh her head off when inside she was terrified. Perhaps she was hysterical after all.

'Well, I do hope so,' Ashok said with a perfectly straight face.

'You have some cheek.' Annie tried to be severe with him.

'Have I passed the test then?' Ashok asked playfully. Annie peered into the screen doubtfully, but Ashok looked back soberly; she could not detect any hint of sarcasm in his demeanour. He really seemed to want to know.

'I am glad that you introduced us,' she replied carefully.

'Good. Now that we have that out of the way, how about letting me have a kiss?' Ashok raised an eyebrow.

'Ashok!' Annie hissed. 'She will hear.'

'She is preparing dinner. Mummy never trusts me to eat properly without her personal supervision.' Ashok grinned unabashedly. 'Can't say I can complain. Do you notice any increase in my weight?'

'I really can't say.' Annie laughed. 'You are incorrigible.'

They chatted for a few more minutes before calling off. Annie felt a surge of excitement in her breast; it was obvious to her now that she had overreacted. Ashok loved her. *He loved her!* She felt like shouting at the top of her voice but called Becky instead. She simply had to share this with somebody.

'Hey! You sound chirpy for sure.' Becky was quick to catch the shift in Annie's voice.

'He loves me, Becky. He loves me, he does,' Annie gushed.

'He does? Of course he does. Why did you doubt in the first place?' Becky laughed with her.

'Oh, I don't know. I am such a miserable wretch. I am so grateful that Ashok is ready to put up with my tantrums. He could easily have shut me out, but he didn't. He introduced me to his mother and—oh, Becky! I am so happy!'

'Steady, girl. Let me take a seat . . . there. Now, tell me all.'

So Annie told her. After listening patiently, Becky had one question. 'What about his father?'

'His father was out. He has said that he will introduce us next time.'

'Hmmm. Okay. Are you happy?'

'I am, oh, I am.' Annie nodded her head vigorously, as if Becky could see her.

'In that case, I am happy for you. Now I have to go before Pixie demolishes my coffee table.'

CHAPTER 26

THINGS FELL INTO A PATTERN after that. Ashok and Annie talked on Skype once a day for at least a quarter of an hour. They would talk about everything under the sun; it seemed that Annie could tell him everything. She talked about her children, her life before Ashok, life with Zack, the abuse she had suffered. The last one made Ashok grim.

'I wish I were there with you, Annie,' he said the first time she mentioned it to him. 'I wish I could be there for you.'

'I am over it now. But it was hell then. The most difficult part was seeing my last son suffer with me,' Annie confessed.

They talked about her work, and she even told him about Gerard. He had called her once or twice after her trip to New York but had gotten the message and laid off. Ashok was not pleased.

'Do you have to work for him? Surely there will be other clients,' he grumbled.

Annie laughed. 'Relax. He is a gentleman. He will never cross the line. Besides, I don't have to actually go and see him often.'

They talked about his work, his ambitions, and his desires. He dreamt of having his own business one day.

'I am trying to learn the trick of the trade as fast as possible. All I now need is some capital, which I expect to get from the banks,' he confided in her. 'How do you think a pan-Indian hotel sounds?'

'It sounds lovely. But do you think it will have many takers in a place called India?' she teased softly.

'It will. That's because I plan to sell it to the foreign tourists that come visiting. You see, there is no India as such. Each region is vastly different—so much so that food from one region is foreign to another. I am thinking of bringing it all under the same roof.'

'Something like the multi-cuisine restaurants in the five-star hotels?'

'Exactly, except you will not find continental or Chinese here, only Indian.'

They talked about everything that came to their minds, except for one thing.

They never talked about their future together.

Hank called before Christmas. The holidays were about to begin; Annie was having a tough time deciding on gifts. This was also the time when she got in touch with everyone, though it was usually limited to phone calls and texting. When Hank called, she was about to go out to the local jewellery store to pick up something for Becky.

'Hello. Mom?'

'Hank!' Annie was surprised. He rarely called. Maybe something was wrong? 'Is everything okay?'

'Everything's fine. I am coming down this Sunday. Thought I'd let you know so that I don't come to an empty house.'

'You did right. I will be there. When are you coming?'

'I am planning to catch the morning flight, so I should be there by mid-morning. Say, around eleven?'

'Splendid. I shall keep lunch ready.'

Annie went out shopping with a broad smile. It was not every day that she got to spend her Sunday with any of the children now that they were grown up and had their own concerns. But it was always a pleasure to see them, especially Hank, who was her firstborn. Sunday could not come fast enough.

Later that day, she mentioned it to Ashok.

'It has put a glow to your face,' Ashok teased.

'I am sure that is not so,' Annie protested.

'Quite noticeable,' Ashok insisted. 'I am glad for you.'

'Yes, it has been some time. Elsa, my daughter, also stays in New York, but she and I never got along. She is a bit self-opinionated . . .' Annie's voice trailed off. She was not sure how Ashok would take that piece of news.

'We all are at one point of time or other to our parents,' Ashok said evenly. 'I am sure she will come around.'

Annie said nothing. She knew that was not to be. Elsa had never taken Annie's guidance in the proper spirit, which she thought was controlling, and terrible fights had ensued. Finally, when Annie had enough of the situation, Elsa simply walked off. Annie had harboured a sliver of guilt, which she had hidden diligently ever since. She wished she could share that with Ashok now, but sitting far away, communicating through an electronic device, she knew this was not the right setting.

'Where are your parents?' she asked instead.

'They have gone to visit the Kali Temple here. It is quite famous. Later they will have dinner with my aunt and then come back late.'

'The aunt who visited Miami?'

'Yeah, that aunt.'

They chatted for a few minutes after that before logging off. Annie had so much to do; she always gave her house a thorough cleaning before Christmas. She finished the living room and the kitchen. Then she went out shopping.

She picked up a cable-knit sweater for Hank in dark-forest green. For one of his girls, she got a pretty silver bracelet, a single charm dangling from one end. For the eldest one, she got her a pair of silver earrings with her birthstone hanging at the end. And for her sister, she bought a red stole, embroidered in black-and-dark-blue satin threadwork. For Nicholas, the youngest, who was still studying, she got a leather-bound edition of baseball cards; he had had a thing for sports since he was young. For Becky, she had a job cut out, for she was expected to pick up gifts for the dogs as well.

Hank arrived before lunchtime on Sunday. He had some business in town and would fly back again Monday evening. Annie had prepared salad and tuna sandwiches with mustard and onion—Hank's favourite.

'This is the best,' Hank remarked, his mouth stuffed with food.

'Don't talk with your mouth full,' Annie rebuked. 'What are you doing for the holidays?'

'I am going up to the mountain lodge of one of my friends. Actually, we three are going together. There will be fishing and a bit of hunting, maybe. The lodge belongs to his family, but they are going there this time of the year, so we are going to have a free run.'

'I thought you would want to spend some time with your wife and kids,' Annie remarked. She poured him some iced tea.

'It's okay with them. They have their own things to do.' Hank took a long swig from the tall glass. 'That was fantastic, Mom. You make the best sandwiches.'

They went out to explore the shops after that, where Hank bought her a knee-length silk dress in silver grey. It had capped sleeves and a full skirt, with a cowl neck. 'You need to go out and have a life,' he remarked when Annie protested that she did not need another dress. 'You are too buried out here.'

'That's not true. I had quite a trip to India earlier this year,' Annie said.

'Yeah, that is all very well. But you need someone to share it with,' Hank observed. 'Visiting places on your own can be half the fun at its best.'

'It sounds funny, coming from you,' Annie said. 'Who is the parent here?'

'Mom, we all have our own lives. What about you? Granted, Zack was the biggest asshole you could find, but I am sure there are better men out there who might be suitable for you.'

'I hope Elsa does not hear you saying that,' Annie said sadly.

Hank shook his head. 'Elsa is not mad at you. Actually, she is not mad, not any more. She just does not know how to come to you after—well, you know. That's all.'

'What is there to know?' Annie was amazed at this piece of news. 'I am her mother. She can come to me whenever she feels like it.'

'I shall tell her that.'

Later, Annie handed him the sweater. 'Will keep me warm in the mountains,' Hank joked. She also gave him the silver bracelet.

'Please give it to Elsa,' Annie requested. 'Tell her that . . .' She suddenly choked, unable to go on. Hank hugged her with one arm, his other arm holding the parcels.

'I will. I will tell her,' he assured her.

Chapter 27

Monday morning saw Hank out of the house after breakfast. He said he would be back for lunch and then would go out again to attend a meeting. He would go straight to the airport from the meeting.

Annie spent the day in her kitchen garden. She liked planting herbs and tomatoes till it was time for her to Skype Ashok. They had established quite a routine, she thought to herself. It was something like being an old married couple, only this was virtual, not real, she reminded herself prosaically. Even then, these daily chat sessions with him were fast becoming her lifeblood; she looked forward to them eagerly.

'So you cooked for your son, did you?' Ashok said teasingly after she told him about the sandwiches.

'I am quite proud of my tuna sandwiches,' Annie agreed.

'Yet when you were with me, pizza it was.' Ashok sighed. Annie could not help laughing at his mock reprimand.

'Oh, come on. You know why,' she said.

'No, I don't know why. Tell me.'

'Ashok,' Annie began when she heard the door key turn. Hank was back.

'Be serious for once. Let me introduce you to Hank. Mind you, he knows nothing about us.'

'Mom?' Hank called loudly from the living room.

'In here, baby,' Annie answered from the bedroom. That was how Hank found her, sitting in the middle of the bed, her laptop opened in front of her.

'Working?' he asked.

'Nope. Come over and say hello to a friend of mine.'

Curious, Hank came over and peered into the screen.

'Hello, Hank,' Ashok said soberly. 'I am Ashok.'

'Hi. I am Hank.'

'Yes, I know. Annie told me about you.'

Hank looked for a long moment at the screen, his face inscrutable. Annie waited anxiously; she wanted Hank and Ashok to like each other.

'She didn't tell me about you, though,' Hank retorted after a moment. Then he moved away from the screen. 'I will be in the spare room. I have to pack. See you later,' he told Annie before moving out of the room.

'That did not go too well, did it?' Ashok said.

Annie was perplexed. 'I am not sure what happened just now. He is normally very polite and friendly. I am sorry, Ashok.'

'Never mind. My parents are leaving in a couple of days. I might be somewhat erratic on the chat, but after that, I shall come back again.'

'You are doing this because of Hank,' Annie said miserably.

'Come on, Annie! Do you really think I am like that? I simply have to be with my parents as they conclude their visit. They do not come here often, you know.'

'Sure. Well, I have to go now. Bye, Ashok. See you later.'

Hank was busy packing his things in his small case when Annie went into the spare room where he had put up for the night.

'What was that for?' she asked without any preamble.

'What was what for?' Hank looked up.

'That piece of rudeness on Skype. I thought I brought you up better than this,' Annie retorted sternly.

'I was not rude.'

'Yes, you were. Care to tell me about it?'

'When you said friend, I expected something else entirely,' Hank confessed.

'You mean . . .'

'Somebody like Becky, yes. More towards your age than mine. Female.' Hank shrugged. 'Maybe,' he amended.

'What do you mean more towards your age? And why did you assume that the friend would be female? What is this? The Middle Ages?'

'Sorry, Mom,' Hank said. He paused in his packing and looked at her straight in the eye. 'You and him—I don't think it is going to work out, Mom. And I am just trying to spare you the pain.' He resumed packing.

Annie was stunned. 'You don't think he is good enough for me?' she asked after a moment of tense silence.

'I don't think he is good for you. Period,' Hank said flatly.

'Really?' Annie could feel her anger rise. 'And what makes you such an authority on human character that you can conclude that after a momentary peek at a computer image?'

'I am not claiming that.' Hank sighed. He pulled close the zipper in his case and turned to look at Annie. 'He is too young for you, Mom. Anybody can see that. He comes from a different place altogether—different culture, different country. I don't think you two have much of a chance. That's all.'

'And I thought I was the parent here.' Annie tried to laugh, but it came out shaky.

Hank came to her and put his arms around her shoulder. He led her to the settee and sat her there, sitting down beside her. Annie hunched her shoulders and clasped her knees with both hands; she felt the weight of the world upon her. Any pleasure she had felt talking to Ashok was gone, she thought dully.

'Mom, I have seen you hurt from a man who didn't deserve you. I was there with you the last time. I don't want you to visit that place again.'

Annie lifted grave eyes to her son. 'Ashok is different. You don't know him. He loves me. I know he does. Why, he came all the way here just to be with me. Nobody has done that for me before, Hank. Nobody.'

'He came all the way from where?'

'India. New Delhi. He works at a hotel there. Oh, Hank, I wish you had been nicer to him.'

'I am sorry. I didn't mean to be rude. Call him back, and I will talk to him again. I will be nicer. I promise.'

'I can't do that. He lives far away. The time difference alone would make it difficult.'

'You mean there are other difficulties as well?' Hank asked, his brow furrowed. 'What are they?'

No, not difficulties, just culture differences. Annie felt uncomfortable. She wished she had not started this conversation. It would be impossible to explain to Hank that Ashok was not at liberty to chat with her any time of the day with his parents, especially his mother, in the house. That would raise too many questions, answers to which she was not ready to share with her son. Not right now anyway as she herself was not sure of the answers.

But Hank was expecting an answer from her.

'He works nightshifts, so he cannot talk for long,' she replied.

'I see.' Hank bent down and kissed her on the cheek. 'I have to get going. Take care, Mom.'

'You too. And talk to Elsa, will you?'

'I will. See you.' He picked up the case and walked out to where the taxi was waiting.

Annie stood for some time in the doorway. Then she closed it behind her and went back to the bedroom. The laptop was sitting on the bed, where she had left it, its lid closed. She went and sat on the bed, her legs crossed. Suddenly she felt dejected, her heart heavy and low. The house felt empty after Hank had left it. True, he had been there for less than twenty-four hours, but his presence was there—lunch to be prepared, the anticipation of seeing him, their easy banter over breakfast, the comforting knowledge of somebody sleeping in the other bedroom. She missed him already. She missed Ashok. How she wished he were there before her, in this room, where she could touch him, smell him, and see the teasing twinkle in his eyes.

She lay back on the bed, staring at the ceiling. Life was becoming more and more drudging every day. The first rush of thrill she had gained with her independence when she had finally broken free of Zack and set up her own business had dulled. Now she knew that she lacked in life. She lacked Ashok, but she could not see a way. There were too many differences between them, and Hank thought he was too young even to be friends with her.

She rolled over to her stomach and closed her eyes.

When she woke up, it was almost dark, and her head felt heavy; she felt depressed. After making a mug of coffee, she carried it over to the work desk in the spare bedroom; she really had to get cracking as a lot of work was pending. Within a few minutes, she was deep into work, busily checking figures and tapping away, her mind totally occupied with the task at hand. She was so concentrated in her work that at first she almost missed the ringing of the phone. It was Ashok.

'Ashok, what are you doing calling me at this hour? It must be almost noon at your place.'

'Just got confirmed. I thought I would share it with you right away.' Ashok sounded excited.

'What is it?' Annie could not help but laugh at his enthusiasm; it was infectious.

'I am visiting Paris for a week starting Wednesday next week,' Ashok said in a rush. 'My company is sending me on a delegation to the international conference on hospitality business there.'

'I am very happy for you,' Annie said indulgently. And it was true; she did feel happy that he was getting to see places even if they were on business trips. She knew he had always wanted to visit various countries—the United States being the first and now France. It seemed that he was finally starting to get what he wanted. But his next words knocked the breath from her lungs.

'I want you to come away with me,' he said.

'What?' She was not sure she had heard him right. 'You mean . . .'

'I mean, I want you to be with me in Paris. I am so looking forward to going there, but I don't want to do it alone. It doesn't feel right. I want to see Paris with you.'

'Oh, Ashok, I don't know what to say.' Annie prevaricated; she was still feeling unsure after Hank's visit.

'Annie, I won't go if you don't.' Ashok sounded firm. Annie bit her lip. She wished they were on Skype; at least she would be able to see his face when he talked.

'Ashok,' she started, but Ashok would not hear anything more.

'It is all settled. I want to see you. It's been too long.' He paused and then said very softly, 'Don't you want to see me, Annie?'

That almost undid her, but she had to stay firm. 'Ashok, I can't drop everything and go. Please understand.'

'I will see you next Wednesday. We shall meet at the Paris International Airport, and then'—he allowed his voice to drop to a sexy drawl—'and then we will go exploring.'

Annie gave a small laugh. 'You are incorrigible.'

'And you love me for it.' His voice suddenly grew sober. 'You do, don't you, Annie? Love me, I mean.'

Annie dropped her head in her hand. 'I love you, Ashok. But I don't know how to go on from there. I sometimes feel so confused.'

'I love you, and you love me. Where is the confusion there, Annie? Now listen carefully. I will be mailing you our flight details. Meet me there as discussed earlier. I've got to go now. Bye.'

He hung up. Annie dropped the phone on the table. One part of her was elated, ecstatic even, that he still thought about her, said he loved her, and wanted to be with her. In Paris. But another part of her, the pragmatic part, felt unsure. She knew that his family ties were strong, and she was not sure if they would accept her in his life. And if they didn't—in fact, she was sure they wouldn't—then would he be there for her still? She was not sure. And she had her children. She did not want a turf war at her doorstep. She wanted each of them to accept Ashok. But she was not sure of Elsa.

She felt life was becoming too complicated.

Annie was not sure what to do with it. She wanted to go, but she was afraid to go. She thought about talking to Becky but sensed this time she was on her own. This was going to be a momentous decision; Becky could not help her in this.

She received her ticket to Paris the next day via email as Ashok had promised.

CHAPTER 28

Paris during Christmastime was magical. Annie felt that as soon as she stepped out of the plane. It was cloudy and dark when she emerged out of the aircraft on to the tarmac, but the city was brightly decked with fairy lights. The airport was lined with blue and red lights that twinkled in the falling dusk. She felt her pulse quicken at the thought of seeing Ashok again, though she knew it would be at least a couple of hours before she actually met him.

Ashok saw her first. His face broke into that gorgeous wide smile he always had, and his whole face seemed to light up as soon as he spotted her among the holiday crowd.

'Annie.' He hurried to her and laid a hand on her shoulder from behind. Annie was startled and whirled around, only to be engulfed in a bear hug, her face muffled in the layers of warm clothing that he had piled on himself. She lifted her face with an effort and managed a weak laugh.

'You look like Nanook of the North,' she said.

Ashok grinned. 'I feel like an Eskimo too but thought it was better to be safe than sorry.'

'It is quite cold, isn't it?'

They talked about the weather for a few minutes as they waited for her luggage to arrive, concentrating on trivialities to hide the intensity of their emotions. Finally, after some time, they managed to pile everything up in a cart and pushed it out of the glass doors.

Annie had never been to Paris before, and she was glad that she was experiencing it for the first time with Ashok. She was struck speechless at the first real sight of the city. By this time, it was completely dark, and the whole place seemed to be lit up. The cars whizzed by—wrong side of the road, she noticed absently—their makes and shapes different from what she was accustomed to at home. The language that flowed around her seemed like music to her ears, people taking in a sing-song tone that she found so sweet. People smiled at her as they passed by; it was magical. And she had Ashok by her side. Annie thought she could want for nothing more in her life at this point.

They got inside the cab. Ashok gave the driver the address and then leaned back on the seat, putting an arm around her shoulder. Annie sighed and leaned her head against him.

'This is magic, isn't it?' she said softly.

'It is, isn't it?'

'Or maybe I am in a dream. In that case, no need to wake me up.'

Ashok squeezed her shoulder. 'Look.' He pointed.

Annie squinted up, and then her mouth fell open. The Eiffel Tower was lit up in all its splendour in hues of gold, mauve, blue, and a myriad other colours.

'I could not even dream of this. This is so . . . it's fairyland,' she said.

'Well, it is the city of the lovers, they say,' Ashok quipped.

They reached the hotel, and the bellboy brought in their luggage. Ashok's company was sponsoring his stay, and he had simply booked a double room, so they did not have to bother with anything. The conference was to be held in the same hotel, so Ashok would not have to commute at all.

They went into the room hand in hand. Annie had decided to push back her doubts. She did not want anything—not even her thoughts—to come between them for these three days. Now, as they stepped into the room together, she was determined to have this week to herself—this very short time that she would have with him in this historic city of lovers.

As soon as she entered the room, she gave a gasp of delight. There were roses everywhere—on the dresser, the small coffee table, the bedside stands. All had pink and white roses in silver-toned vases. She dropped her purse on the floor and, on an impulse, whirled around and threw her arms around Ashok's neck.

'This is so beautiful. I never imagined it would be so beautiful. Thank you.' She kissed him full on his lips.

Ashok laughed. 'I have not done anything, dear. This is part of my requested decor just for you.' He tipped the bellboy and closed the door softly behind him. 'Now, where were we?' he said in a low voice. He pulled Annie urgently—almost roughly—into his arms, his lips descending on hers. They kissed as if they wanted to devour each other; they had been starved for each other for too long. Soon, their clothes were piled on the floor, their hands moving urgently as if reacquainting with each other as they made passionate love. Everything else could wait; loving each other could not.

Later, they showered together. Ashok insisted on lathering her down and almost smothered her in copious amounts of foam. They laughed hysterically before they rinsed off and towelled themselves dry. Ashok had ordered room service for dinner. The waiter rolled the trolley in as Annie was drying her hair. When she came into the room, she stopped right in the doorway.

'Oh my god!' she exclaimed. 'This is beautiful.'

The trolley was laden with silver-covered dishes, a bunch of white roses serving as the centrepiece. The water jug and the glasses were of heavy crystal, sparkling under the light.

'Come on. I am famished,' Ashok said. Annie thought he sounded a bit terse, but she said nothing.

The food was delicious. 'I have heard about French cuisine, but I never thought it would be this good,' she remarked as they ate.

'They are known for their gourmet delights,' Ashok concurred. 'But I personally find it a bit too bland.'

'Hmm, you would, after what I have seen about the food in India.'

They polished off the plates, and then Annie suddenly yawned. 'Sorry,' she apologized.

'You shouldn't be,' Ashok said. 'It has been a long journey for both of us, and what with the exercise we had right after'—he winked at her—'it is natural to feel tired. I think we should go to bed.'

'I really do feel sleepy,' Annie admitted. She laid her head on his chest as his arms wrapped around her, and they both fell asleep.

The next morning, Ashok had a couple of hours on his hands before he was required at the conference, so they decided to explore the city a bit. They went out early in the morning, planning to have breakfast at one of the roadside cafes that dotted Paris. Afterwards, they went to the riverside. Annie wanted to tie a love lock on the bridge, but she found out that it can no longer be done as they became too many and a danger to the bridge. They instead spent some time watching the ferries on the river for a while, and then Ashok had to go back to the hotel. Annie decided she wanted to see more of the city—she was completely enchanted by it—and Ashok took a taxi back.

When Annie came back to the hotel, it was already past lunchtime. She had a sandwich, part of which she fed to the ducks at a park, and went straight up to her room. Ashok had told her that he would be back by evening, so she had some time on her hands. She wanted to have a spa and massage but was not sure of how expensive it would be; she was not sure of the exchange rate. She went down to the reception to enquire.

The lobby was full of people—from the conference, she deduced. There seemed to be people from all regions and races; it was an international conference after all. She talked to the reception clerk, and after much gesticulating and laughter on both sides, she finally got the information she wanted. As she turned back to go to the spa, she spotted Ashok. He was talking to a group of people at the far end of the lobby. Among the group was a woman. She was blonde, about thirty years old, reed thin, and superbly glamorous. She was smiling towards Ashok in a way that made Annie want to rip out her hair right there and then. She averted her face and hurried in the direction of the spa.

While she lay under the therapist's expert hands, her mind went busy. Ashok was an extremely attractive man who could have any woman he wanted. The way the woman smiled at him was an example of that. So why did he even want to be with her? Maybe he was telling her the truth— that he loved her. Dare she believe him? But what about afterwards? Ashok would go back to India, and she would go back to the States. They would not see each other for weeks, months even. She could hardly expect him to stay celibate all those times they were apart. The thought of him with another woman, in whatever capacity, brought such a spurt of distress inside her that she actually groaned. The therapist was startled.

'Madam, in pain?' she asked.

'No—I mean yes, but not the kind you think,' Annie replied, smiling to reassure her.

'Maybe I can do it lighter?'

'No. No, please. Do go on. I love it.'

CHAPTER 29

WHEN SHE CAME BACK TO the lobby, the group was gone. She knew she had to go up to her room and get changed but was not really looking forward to it. The city outside beckoned her, bright and colourfully lit up for the holidays. It occurred to her that she had not bought anything for Ashok. She had thought about him while shopping back home but was not sure that he would want a Christmas gift, seeing that he was not a Christian. But now she wished she had something for him. She decided to go out and look at the shops that lined the streets.

She picked up a silk tie for him at one of the many stores lining the streets of the city. After that, she went browsing in the tiny gift shops, looking for little knick-knacks to carry back home. It was a couple of hours before she stopped to have some coffee at one of the street-side cafes. After that, she went back to the hotel.

The lobby was deserted, except for a few tourists lingering over coffee and drinks. She was famished after her long trek on the streets, so she hurried to her room, intent to change before dinner. Ashok must have been wondering about her, she thought. She smiled a little to herself, thinking about his reaction to her gift for him. She wanted to take a shower before she changed into something really good—for his eyes only.

'Where the hell have you been?' Ashok was waiting in the room and hissed furiously as soon as she entered.

'Out. Shopping.' Annie was taken aback by his reaction. 'Were you back a long time? I bought you a gift.'

'Out? Shopping? That is all you have to say? Do you realize I have been waiting here for almost an hour?'

'Well, I am sorry. But how was I to know that?' Annie crossed over to the dresser and put the purchases on top.

Ashok got up from where he was sitting by the French windows. 'You just left without so much as a message. What was I supposed to do? I had no idea where you were, where you'd gone,' he fumed.

'Well, excuse me.' Annie felt her own anger rising. 'I did not realize that I was to report to you every time I stepped out of the hotel.'

'Yes, you should. You should at least text me so that I know that . . .'

'Know what, Ashok?' Annie drew herself to her full height. 'Kindly remember that I am a grown woman who has been taking care of herself for a long time now. I *do not* report to anybody—even you. I will go out if I please, thank you. You simply have to trust me to do the right thing and come back safely. Thank you. Now, if you will excuse me, I will have my shower.'

Having said her piece, she marched off into the bathroom, not allowing Ashok to see the sudden tears that welled up.

Once inside, she took off her clothes, adjusted the temperature, and stepped under the jet of water. It felt soothing, even though her limbs were still trembling after the ugly exchange with Ashok. Why was he being so proprietorial all of a sudden? Memories haunted her—of a man shouting, demanding that she stay at home and not step out. He was the master of the house and expected her to go by the laws he lay down. God, was he like Zack after all? What was the matter with her? Would she be doomed for the rest of her life, falling for the wrong kind of man?

The soap was taken away from her hand. Strong arms came around her, turning her gently so that she faced the wall of the shower stall. Ashok started to soap her back in long, even strokes, which felt so good that she sighed. He did not say a word. Instead, he soaped every inch of her, including her hair, which he shampooed. Then he rinsed them both before turning off the shower and stepping out of it, taking her along with him.

Annie followed him meekly, inwardly cringing for giving in so easily.

'I am sorry,' Ashok said in a low voice. 'I came back and saw you were not here. Tried calling you, and it went to voicemail. I panicked. This is a foreign country, and I didn't know what to do if anything would have happened to you.'

Annie frowned and went to the dresser. She fished inside her purse and brought up the cell phone. It was dead. The battery must have gone out while she was shopping. Dropping the phone, she came back to him, putting her arms around his neck.

'No, I am sorry. I should have checked my phone before going out. I didn't stop to think, went out on an impulse. I just—I wanted to give you something. It is Christmastime, and I wanted to buy you a gift.'

'So show me your gift.' Ashok grinned.

She brought out the dark-blue silk tie with tiny anchors in black printed all over it.

'I love it.' Ashok smiled. 'Thank you.' He bent down and kissed her full on her lips. 'Now, who wants dinner?'

Half an hour later, they went down to the restaurant at the hotel.

The rest of the time in Paris seemed like a dream to Annie. They had their meals together, often outside the hotel at Annie's insistence, for she wanted to explore the city as much as they could. They went on a tour down the Seine and then had a peek at the Louvre, but it was too much for one day. While Ashok attended his conference, Annie went out by herself. She loved to have coffee by the roadside, watching young art students sketching by the river, taking walks along the narrow cobbled streets of the older part of the city. They would have delicious French wine with their food at lunch, Ashok complaining about feeling fuzzy at the meetings but laughing nonetheless.

They had some time on their hands the last evening as Ashok's conference ended sooner than expected. Annie was delighted.

'Let us go and see the Eiffel,' she said excitedly.

'We have already done that,' Ashok murmured.

'But not while it is lit up in the evening. The whole place lights up in different colours, you know. Oh, please do let us go.'

'You are such a child,' Ashok indulged. They took a cab and went.

Once there, they decided to take the ride up. Annie insisted that it would be a life-altering experience.

'It is a little bit like the Qutb Minar, isn't it?' Ashok remarked as they went up the elevator. 'Only much higher, and of course, we don't have the elevator.'

'That is because it is much older than this,' Annie said. 'Elevators weren't invented then.'

As they went up to the topmost viewing deck, both of them fell silent. The city of Paris was spread out before them with its historical landmarks. They could spot Notre Dame, Versailles, the river cutting through the middle of the city.

'Oh my god!' Annie gasped softly. 'This is so beautiful.' She turned misty eyes towards Ashok, who gazed ahead of him in awestruck wonder. 'Thank you.'

Ashok looked at her, startled. 'What for?'

'For insisting that I come to Paris with you. Otherwise, who knows?' She shrugged. 'I might never have seen this.'

Without a word, Ashok hugged her close with one hand around her shoulders, and they turned together to drink in the view against the setting sun on the other side of the river. They could not end this romantic evening without stopping at the 58 Tour Eiffel restaurant for a light French dinner; they took a table for two next to the wide, spanning windows with a panoramic view overlooking the Trocadéro area of Paris.

That night, their lovemaking had a different quality than Annie had ever experienced before. Ashok was gentler, caring somehow, which increased the intensity of her pleasure to a height that was almost unbearable. Afterwards, she lay awake on the bed, her head on his chest, as he slept. This seemed to be their way of falling asleep every night. She wished Ashok had been awake with her. As she listened to his gentle snoring, it occurred to her that Ashok had been strangely melancholic while making love. She wondered why. Oh, it had been totally blissful, as always, but there was a lingering quality in his movements. She really could not put her finger on it, but it returned to haunt her now. It was almost as if he regretted—what, she was not sure. She lay with her eyes open for a long time, looking at the fairy lights blinking outside on the streets until her eyelids grew heavy, and she slept.

They left Paris the following day. Ashok caught an early morning flight, while Annie waited for a couple of hours more at the airport for her flight to New York. As she watched him go through the departure gate, she felt her stomach hit the floor when he turned back just before he disappeared and blew her a kiss. She stretched out her hands and caught it with a smile and touched her lips. Was she ever going to get used to missing him this much? Did he miss her as much as she missed him? The thought of going back to her empty house filled her with dread. She decided on an impulse to visit Hank in New York before she went home to Miami.

CHAPTER 30

NEW YORK WAS CROWDED AND as busy as ever. Hank was happy to hear from her, but he was with his friends at the cabin already. Annie was happy for him but a bit sad that she was going to spend Christmas alone after all. All her children had their own plans; Elsa was out of touch, but the other two, her younger ones, planned to spend it with their friends. Annie felt depressed among the festivities in the city.

'Lonely in a crowd, is it? Come on, you are pathetic. Get a grip,' she told herself sternly. But the feeling remained.

It was already dark when she got back home. 'What is he doing now?' she wondered. She imagined him flying cross the ocean—he would still be on his flight—then gave up as it made her want to cry. She put down her luggage in the bedroom and went to find the fairy lights instead. She had long given up on the tree but still decorated her house and the lawn with the lights. This year, hers was the only house not lit up on the street.

'That would not do,' she muttered to herself.

A couple of hours later, the house was a twinkling fairy house. Satisfied, Annie immediately fell into a deep, dreamless sleep without having had dinner.

Christmas Day arrived bright and sunny. Annie got up early and had a breakfast of muesli and coffee. Becky called.

'Hi there. What is my favourite girl doing?'

Annie burst into tears.

'Hey, girl. What's the matter, love?' Becky was concerned.

'He has not called. It's been three days since, Becky. I don't know what to do.'

'Ashok? Well, there are so many reasons why he might not have called, love. Why don't you call him and find out?'

'I can't. How can I?'

'If you love him, you can, Annie,' Becky said gravely. 'Maybe he wants to but cannot for some reason. Have you considered that possibility?'

Annie's fear grew after that conversation. Maybe he was sick. Or worse. She decided to call him after coming back from church.

Later, after she was back from church, the local ladies' committee members came calling. They were organizing a small raffle for New Year's and wanted her to participate in it. Annie really did not want to but could not say no as that would be rude. She promised to bake some cookies and attend the raffle. After they were gone, she looked around the house. Her Christmas presents lay in a heap on the living room coffee table. She sat down and started to open them one by one. Hank had sent her a silk scarf in brilliant hues of red and black. Chocolates, mittens, a CD of her favourite jazz artist from children. Elsa had sent a pink sweater. One look at it, and she knew she was never going to wear it, but she would cherish it as her rebel child had at least thought about her this time of the year. Becky had sent her a silver anklet. She smiled as she put it on. It had tiny coloured beads that glittered as she turned her ankle this way and that to see how it looked. Her parents had sent her a pair of woollen socks and a matching cap in light blue and silver grey. She made a mental note to remind her mother that she was no longer five! But she was glad that they were well and happy, and in her heart, she knew that she loved the gifts.

She opened the last box with trembling hands. Ashok had given it to her on their last night at Paris. They had made love, and he suddenly got out of bed and rummaged through his open suitcase, coming back with the tiny box. It was wrapped in silver paper, with a blue ribbon tied neatly around it.

'You cannot open it now. Open it on Christmas Day,' he had said.

Now, as she opened the silver paper, she was almost afraid of what she would find.

Inside, nestled among the blue velvet, was a delicate gold chain with an oval pendant. The centre was a pearl with tiny diamonds around it. It was exquisite. Slowly she lifted it up against the light; it seemed to glow in the bright morning sun, with the diamonds twinkling merrily. She put it around her neck and rushed to the mirror to have a look. It nestled just under her collarbone, the warm creamy pearl complementing her tanned skin.

On an impulse, she picked up the phone and dialled before she lost her nerve. Glancing at her watch, she figured it would be late night but not too late to call.

Ashok picked up after the ninth ring. 'Merry Christmas, Annie,' he responded even before she said her first hello.

'Merry Christmas. I just opened your present. Ashok, it is beautiful. I have never received anything so beautiful in my life. Thank you.'

'I am glad you like it.'

'Why didn't you call?' Annie blurted out.

'I am working now, Annie. This is one of the busiest times of the year for us, you know. Can we have this conversation later?'

'Yes, of course. I am sorry. I just wanted to say thank you.'

'You are welcome. Bye, Annie.'

'Bye, Ashok.'

Annie was completely confused and not a little scared. What was the matter? Why did he sound so cold? Maybe he did not want to have anything to do with her after all. Maybe he . . . she could not think any further. Dropping down on the bed, she cried her heart out.

She went to the church dinner in the evening. She wore the indigo dress she had bought in India, the pearl-and-diamond pendant nestling against her throat. Come what may, she had decided to cherish this one Christmas present and wear it always for the rest of her life. Even as people laughed and raised their glasses in cheers, Annie remained stoic amongst it all, with a heavy heart.

Becky called the next day. She was on a cruise.

'I am glad that you are enjoying your cruise so much,' Annie said. 'You deserve it.'

'What is the matter, darling? Is everything all right?' her friend asked at once. Annie was speechless. Even after all these years, her friend could discern her distress. She did not need to hear the words. Her voice would be enough. She knew pretending was of no use, so she told her everything. She told her about her meeting with Ashok, her love for him, his recent withdrawal, and the last one bringing tears to her eyes.

'I am sorry that you are on your own, Annie,' Becky said. 'Nobody should be alone during Christmastime. Maybe you can join me on the ship?'

'Oh, Becky.' Annie laughed through her tears. 'You know I can't do that. Besides, I will see you when you get back on Friday.'

They talked a few minutes after that, and then they rang off.

There was no call or any communication from Ashok. Becky arrived on Friday, along with her dogs. They spent time watching old movies on DVDs and having huge platters of fritters, which Becky insisted on preparing.

'You will make me fat. I am sure of that,' Annie complained.

'Nonsense. This is better than wallowing in tubs of ice cream,' Becky countered.

CHAPTER 31

ASHOK CALLED HER ON SUNDAY. It was evening, and
Becky had gone out to rent new DVDs when he called
to say that he would be on Skype. Annie rushed to the
laptop, and sure enough, he was there.

The first thing she noticed about him was that he looked
thinner; his lips were drawn in grim lines.

'Are you okay?' she asked anxiously, her angst forgotten
in her concern for him.

Ashok nodded. 'I have a few minutes before going to
work, so I thought I would talk to you.'

'You did right.'

'Why are you in your nightie?' Ashok asked suddenly.

'What—' Annie looked down at herself in confusion.
She was wearing an old robe as she intended to spend the
day relaxing. Now she went red in embarrassment. 'Oh, I
was just . . .' Her voice trailed away.

'You look charming anyway.' Ashok grinned suddenly.
Then he went grave again. 'I wish I were with you now.'

'I wish that too,' Annie said softly.

'I am going through a crisis, Annie. I thought to spare you all this, but it seemed unfair. You deserve to know.'

'What is it, Ashok? You can tell me everything. You know that,' Annie said even as her heart sank. Something was wrong. She just knew it.

'I met this girl—no, that started badly. Actually, my parents made me meet this girl. They want me to marry her.'

Annie felt herself grow cold all over. 'Please elaborate,' she said in a calm voice. She knew what he was saying but would be damned if she allowed him to see what it did to her.

'Yes, of course. This girl, she is from a family known to my mother, and she and her mother want us to get married.'

'An arranged marriage.'

'It is quite common here. You know that. I have known her since I was a boy, actually.'

'So you knew that you were going to marry her and spent time with me anyway. A fling on the side, was I?' Annie was unable to keep the bitterness from her voice. Inside, she felt as if she were crumbling into a thousand pieces.

'You have met my aunt. You have seen how conservative they are, and . . .'

'Of course. I would be impossible for you. I see that. A woman older than you, a foreigner of a different religion . . . you don't have to explain. Congratulations, by the way,' Annie said softly before putting down the lid of the laptop.

She sat on the bed for a long, long time—until Becky came home anyway. She went through the motions automatically—watching the movies, laughing on cue, cuddling the dogs, going about as if everything was all right. Except it was all wrong.

It was much worse this time. She felt betrayed. By herself. She had nobody to blame. Earlier, she had been too young or too desperate. With Zack, she was already a single mother of four; she had clutched on to him in desperation, refusing to see the signs that were so obvious to others. This time, she had no such excuse. She was a mature, independent woman who had allowed herself to be used by the most suave man on earth like a stupid, naive fool.

She could not even bring herself to tell Becky.

Her phone rang when she was preparing for bed. It was Ashok. She put the handset on silent mode and took two sleeping tablets, knocking herself into a heavy, drugged sleep.

The days fell into a pattern from that day on. She would spend time with Becky, who had decided to stay until New Year, and would make herself oblivious to the gnawing pain that ate away at her the whole day with medication at night.

New Year came and went. Annie baked a whole batch of cookies and went to the raffle. Becky was charmed by the coloured tents and frilled stalls. She contributed home-made tarts. It was late when they came back. Annie ached all over from standing at the stalls the whole day. She welcomed the pain though. It kept her mind off Ashok. Even after what he had done, she missed him terribly and wished he were with her. She was angry with herself for her weakness, but there she was.

Becky left the next day. Annie felt as if the empty house would swallow her up; the doors looked like wide-jawed mouths of some unknown monsters.

I shall go mad if I go on like this, she thought to herself.

She decided to throw herself in her work. She hardly raised her head from the computer, taking very short breaks only when she felt hunger pains. She would fix herself a quick sandwich and go back right to work, eating as she typed away. Sometimes she took long walks along the beach. She found that the sound of the gently lapping waves soothed her.

Hank called. He had come back from his hike in the mountains. She was glad to hear his voice, but his youthful exuberance opened up her raw wounds somehow. That night, she cried herself to sleep after a long time.

Days passed. January gave in to February. Annie felt no better. Maybe he had married and moved on, she thought. The thought brought such a flood of overwhelming grief that her legs almost gave away beneath her. It was stupid though, for he had made it quite clear that Annie had been no more than a diversion while his demure, virginal bride waited for the right time to step in.

She turned off the stove and stepped out. She needed air, badly.

She went to the beach. It was almost sundown, and Annie loved to see the sun go down while she took her walks. She walked longer than usual, trying to come to terms with the longings in her heart that refused to listen to her mind. It was quite dark when she began her trek home.

Spring came in due time, flooding the town with tropical flowers and fresh greenery. It brought no joy to Annie; she went on with her days with the same stoic grimness as before. She thought less about Ashok every day, even if she was not aware of it. But she had yet to forgive herself for falling in love with him. She wished she had treated it as a summer fling too; it would certainly be the more mature thing to do. She saw that now. But she had not, and it had broken her heart into a thousand pieces in the process. She had nobody to blame, no matter how much it hurt. Sometimes she wondered what would have happened if she were not a foreigner to his family, if she were younger and nearer his age. Most likely, she would have been married off to the nearest bidder and never met Ashok, she thought pragmatically. And yet . . .

She was working late into the night—she worked late nowadays, sleeping little—when the call came.

At first, she tried to ignore it, for it was really late and also because she was deep into her work and resented the distraction. Then it occurred to her that somebody might be trying to reach out with some important news. Her attention was on the screen before her, and she took the call without checking the caller.

'Annie?'

The deep voice almost stopped her heart. She took a deep breath before answering.

'Ashok. Hi.'

'How are you, Annie?'

'I am fine.' Pride dictated no other answer. 'How are you?'

Ashok sighed. 'I am going through a crisis, and you are the first person I thought of. I hope you don't mind my calling you like this.'

'Not at all,' Annie replied coolly. 'I hope it is not too bad.'

'It is as bad as it can get, Annie. My wife just walked out on me. She wants a divorce.'

'I am sorry.' Annie was stunned. She was not expecting this. Why was he calling her anyway? She decided to ask him. 'Why are you calling though, Ashok?'

'Do you want to know why she left, Annie?' Ashok said heavily. Annie found that she didn't want to know. It suddenly felt sordid somehow. She was not going to pry into his marriage.

'I don't, actually. But I am sure you will have the right solution,' she said.

'She left', Ashok continued as if she had not spoken, 'because she found out that I loved another woman.'

Now Annie felt definitely uncomfortable. 'I am truly sorry, but it has got nothing to do with me.'

'Doesn't it? Seeing that you are the woman I love.'

'You should not say such things, Ashok. Not any more,' Annie said sadly. She felt sad but little else, which was much to her surprise. A couple of months back, this would have been music to her ears, but now, all she felt was a deep sadness at what could have been. 'You should try to mend the differences with your bride. She is insecure, and she is hurting.'

'I do not wish to mend things with her,' Ashok said.

Annie felt a spark of anger at him. 'Well, that is tough. You have to work to have a marriage, you know. Take this from somebody who knows. And as for your love for me, I appreciate that. I really do. But it is not to be, Ashok. We are too apart—too different to make it work.'

'But, Annie,' Ashok protested.

'No, listen to me,' Annie continued. 'I love you too. I will always do so, I think. But marriage, that is a long journey. Love is not enough, at least most of the time. I will never forget you, but I think we are better off like this.'

'Can I call you from time to time? Will you take my calls?' Ashok wanted to know.

'I will always cherish your calls, Ashok. Knowing that you are out there, in another part of the world, thinking of me is what will keep me going. Believe that.'

'Please don't ever give up on me. Just give me time to sort all this out. I promise we will find our way back. I love you,' Ashok said softly. 'Please don't ever doubt that.'

'And I love you too, always will. Bye, Ashok.'

Annie hung up with a decisive click. Her heart felt heavy, but to her relief, that agonizing pain was not there any more. She felt as close to happy as she ever would be, she supposed. She loved him still, but it was a more gentle feeling, like a dearly treasured friend, somebody who was always present in her mind but not in the everyday fabric of her existence. And she realized too that she preferred it this way. It was less painful. She had enough of intense, all-consuming passion to last her a lifetime.

She peered into the numbers on the laptop screen. Numbers were safe; they were her friends. They never betrayed, she thought, as she tapped busily on the keys. There was a deadline to finish after all.

After the final conservation with Ashok, Annie thought about the word *love* and what it really meant and began pounding away on the laptop about that word that was used so loosely.

What Is Love

Love is really undefined. If you could define it, then where would the mystery be? It's something that is a common bond between two people who feel like they need each other to survive. It's more than just the feeling and sincerity of the word. Love is not lust. It doesn't have a preference—black, white, gay, straight, or age difference. The feeling is more than the human mind can comprehend. Love makes you feel warm and fuzzy inside. It gives you butterflies in your stomach. It makes you weak in the knees and your palms sweaty. It makes it hard to focus on anything but that person. It's a feeling—an effect you get caught up in. When you're in love, you can't define reality from your heart. Love is the reason why people stay so strong. Love keeps people wanting what they can't always have. Love is complicated beyond belief but also wonderful beyond belief. True love always hurts. It truly can hurt for long periods of time. Love makes you go insane to be with that person, and they become your high.

Some say love doesn't last forever. I believe it does. Love between two people who are stubborn enough beyond all consequences take charge and take chances. Love is not a risk; it's the reward. Love is wanting nothing but to love and be loved and finally be happy. Love is unconditional, having that strong feeling regardless of circumstance or characteristics— loving someone when you don't even know why you do or even when you know they don't deserve it. You can't control it. It is there whether you like it or not. It is unexplainable, but if it could be explained, it would be something like this: love is a feeling beyond what you've imagined. It's waking up in the morning and thinking of your significant other. It's that thought, that touch, that togetherness that you have right before bed that makes you happy.

They make you happy just thinking about them. Love is giving your everything and your all; it's an emotional feeling. It's not something you buy in order to be happy. It's an emotion that hits you suddenly in the gut without any warning, and as I said, love has no bounds!

ABOUT THE AUTHOR

SARAH ROBERTS IS A TRAVELLER who loves to explore new and exotic places. She has worked in the travel business for more than twenty years.

Through her professional career in travel, she helps travellers plan their vacations. Family reunions, retreats, weddings, romantic getaways, and cruising are her specialties. As a travel consultant with the largest vacation retailer in the United States, Sarah takes people to the world and beyond. She makes your dreams come true, guarantee exceptional, and top-notch personal service every step of the way.

When she isn't working, we can find her taking pictures with the camera her friend gave her for her trip. She also loves reading and watching television to learn more about the world. Fiercely independent and a true explorer, she is passionate about life and enjoys being free.

In her new book, *Under the Indian Sun*, Sarah takes readers on a personal journey through Delhi, Jaipur, Agra, and finding love during her tour of India.

Printed in the United States
By Bookmasters